THE WOMAN WITHOUT A WORLD

THE WARLORD – BOOK #1

BY M. D. COOPER

Cover Art by Ravven
Editing by Jen McDonnell

TABLE OF CONTENTS

FOREWORD

I have always wanted to write more about the events which occurred during the years the *Intrepid* spent at Kapteyn's Star. Far more went on in that timeframe than ever made it into Building Victoria.

Someday I will tell those stories: the work that went into building a stable world around a red dwarf star, how the peoples integrated, and then eventually split, tales of the young men and women who joined Joe's academy, and later became the backbone of the Intrepid Space Force.

Kapteyn's Star was the crucible that forged Tanis and her people into a force that could withstand what came after they passed through the Streamer.

Had it not been for the bravery of one man—Markus of the Noctus—who stood up to oppression and led the *Hyperion* to Kapteyn's Star, Tanis and the *Intrepid* would not have been strong enough to survive the Battle of the Five Fleets at Bollam's World.

But there was another person who was instrumental in those trying times—without whom Markus would have failed. And with his failure would have come the loss of the *Intrepid* in the far future.

That woman, standing at the side of the stage and ensuring that all proceeded as it should, was Katrina.

This brave woman stayed behind after the *Intrepid* left for New Eden, supposedly lost in the winds of time, her part played.

Or perhaps not….

PREVIOUSLY IN THE INTREPID SAGA

In the year 4230, after suffering damage from saboteurs at Estrella de la Muerte, the *Intrepid* arrived in the Kapteyn's Star System to make repairs.

The system was supposedly uninhabited, but as the *Intrepid* approached, its crew discovered that a ship of refugees from the Sirius System was also inbound.

Under General Tanis Richards' guidance, the colonists aboard the *Intrepid* helped the refugees settle the worlds around Kapteyn's Star.

During the seventy years that the two groups shared The Kap, they fended off three separate attacks from the Sirians, who were seeking revenge against the refugees. The aggression culminated in the Battle of Victoria, where the Intrepid Space Force defeated a much larger Sirian fleet by unleashing their superweapon, the picoswarm bomb.

The victory was total, and it was believed that The Kap would be safe from future aggression.

In 4304, twelve years after that final battle, the *Intrepid* left The Kap, resuming its journey to the New Eden System where the Future Generation Terraformers still waited to greet the colonists.

Before the *Intrepid* left The Kap, they assisted in creating a new stellar government where each planet, moon, and major station had a voice. This new stellar nation was named The Kapteyn Primacy.

One of the Primacy's first actions was to create the Veil Act; a law whose purpose was to ensure that the Kap System appeared uninhabited and unworthy of notice.

Not long after the ratification of the Veil Act, the *Intrepid* failed to send its one-year-status message.

Katrina, the last of the original generation of refugees from Sirius, was still in her final year as the President of the world of Victoria when this occurred. She pushed to have a scout ship sent out, but her efforts were in vain.

And so a second year of silence from the *Intrepid* passed.

When the Primacy finally did send a ship out in search of the *Intrepid,* they found nothing. The scout ship searched fruitlessly for two years before being recalled.

Some people of the Primacy had family members on the *Intrepid,* and they petitioned long and hard to send a larger search effort, but were ultimately denied.

The new government did not want to violate the Veil Act they had just enacted; they also did not want to alert the terraformers waiting at New Eden that anything was wrong. If the terraformers believed that the *Intrepid* was lost, they would grant the system to a new group of colonists.

And so the Primacy's official policy was set. They would wait.

When this decision was made, the *Intrepid*'s projected arrival at New Eden was still fifty-six years hence. With the nine years it would take for the arrival message to reach The Kap, it would be another sixty-five years before the people of Kapteyn's Primacy learned of the *Intrepid*'s fate.

Katrina was not prepared to wait sixty-five years.

In defiance of the Primacy and the Veil Act, Katrina sent a message to New Eden where the terraformers still waited, praying that they had news from the *Intrepid,* praying that the great ship was safe.

LOST

STELLAR DATE: 04.11.4330 (Adjusted Gregorian)
LOCATION: Katrina's Quarters, High Victoria
REGION: Victoria, Kapteyn Primacy, Kapteyn's Star System

"How much longer?" Katrina asked as she settled down at her kitchen table, coffee in hand.

<*We've passed the time needed for a round trip,*> Troy replied over the Link. <*We could get a reply at any moment, or it could take days, even months. You know this.*>

"Dammit, I know," Katrina swore. "This is killing me. Stars' light, where could they be? What could have happened to them?"

Troy didn't respond, which was unusual for the AI. Perhaps he was feeling more anxious than he let on. Or it could be that the question wasn't a new one, and the conversation that typically followed had become old and tired years ago.

It had been twenty-six years since the *Intrepid* had gone silent. Twenty-six long years of waiting and worry.

Laura entered the kitchen and placed a hand on Katrina's shoulder. "I take it no word has come yet?"

Katrina shook her head. "Not yet, but it's been enough time. We should hear back at any moment now."

Laura smiled and leaned over to place a chaste kiss on Katrina's cheek. "I'll make you a sandwich—it'll give me something to do at least. What do you want, Kat?"

"A BLT," Katrina replied. It seemed fitting.

Watching Laura prepare the meal was a welcome distraction. Her personal assistant was a lovely young woman. Full of life and excitement, but very conscientious and exacting. It was why Katrina had chosen her from all of the applicants when her old assistant had passed away seven years ago.

Over that time, Laura had become a close confidant, and eventually, Katrina had shared with her the knowledge that she had violated the Primacy's Veil Act and sent a message to the terraformers at New Eden.

Laura made a BLT for herself as well and, after topping off Katrina's coffee, sat down to eat with her. Afterward, they played a game of cards, and then Laura rose to put the dishes in the wash, while Katrina rose to pace.

She had not taken three steps when Troy called out.

<Jerome got the message!> Troy's mental tone was more excited than he had been for years. *<He picked it up on the edge of the system and successfully purged it from the sensor net. Routing it to you.>*

Katrina felt the message hit her mind, and then a man's face appeared in her vision. He was young, something which surprised Katrina. The *Destiny Ascendant,* the ship that had been tasked with terraforming the worlds of New Eden, had left Sol over five hundred years ago.

Their senior leadership—those she expected to respond to her message—should be quite old by this point; unless they had already passed on, and a new generation was in command.

Katrina suspected that she would never know for sure. The FGT ships were secretive and rarely communicated with anyone anymore; the fact that they had responded to her was a miracle in and of itself.

"Hello, my name is Assistant Director Huron of the FGT Worldship *Destiny Ascendant.* I regret that Director Kallias is not present to respond to you. She long ago took the *Ascendant* on to our next assigned system."

That made sense. The FGT Worldship didn't need to wait for the *Intrepid*. It would appear that Assistant Director Huron had drawn the short straw, and likely waited for the *Intrepid* with a skeleton crew.

"Your message troubles us greatly, and we're dismayed that the captain of the *Intrepid* has misled us in his communications regarding their delays. That being said, it is quite fascinating that they worked with you to terraform the Kapteyn's Star system—we may send someone to view the work you've done."

<*He's equivocating,*> Troy said. <*The news isn't good.*>

Katrina nodded slowly, remaining silent as Assistant Director Huron continued.

"We had already sent out a scout ship in search of the *Intrepid,* and turned our arrays toward the Kapteyn's Star System, but there is no sign of the ship—neither whole, or otherwise."

The assistant director paused for a moment and his expression grew sorrowful. "I don't know what to tell you, President Katrina. The darkness between the stars is a dangerous place—no one knows this better than the FGT. We will continue to search for any sign of the *Intrepid,* but I fear the worst.

"I must also send a message to Director Kallias. There are protocols for ships that do not arrive, and the *Intrepid* will soon reach the end of their extensions. When that happens, we will have to rescind their colony grant and inform the Generation Ship Service in Sol that New Eden is once more accepting colony applic—"

Katrina stopped the playback. She had no desire to hear whatever else the man had to say. His apology was genuine, but all he had done was create more questions.

Laura had silently waited as Katrina watched the message. When it was done, the young woman spoke quietly. "Your eyes have told me all I need to know."

Katrina shook her head. "It is as I feared."

"Will you bring this to the Primacy, then?" Laura asked, her tone soft and wavering. "Or will you leave us?"

Katrina walked toward Laura and placed a hand on her arm. "You know the answer to that. My time here is over." She looked up and closed her eyes. "Will you come, Troy?"

<*What do you think, Katrina? I was going eventually, no matter what. What's your plan? I assume you have one.*>

APPEAL

STELLAR DATE: 07.13.4330 (Adjusted Gregorian)
LOCATION: Landfall Capitol Buildings, Landfall
REGION: Victoria, Kapteyn Primacy, Kapteyn's Star System

Katrina sat patiently outside of President Leanne's office—an office that had been hers some decades earlier.

It always felt strange to be the one out here, forced to wait on another's pleasure while they dealt with matters of state. Sometimes—not often, but sometimes—she wished to be back in that room. On the other side of the desk.

There were so many things she would do differently…

"The President is ready for you now, Matrem Katrina," the man sitting at the desk next to the door said.

"Thank you," Katrina answered, rising slowly and fighting the stiffness in her knees from sitting too long. At only two hundred and eight years, Katrina should not be feeling her age this much; but she had forgone rejuvination for some time, wanting to age as gracefully as she could alongside her late husband.

An age she had retained in memory of Markus.

What would you do, Markus? Katrina sent the question off into the ether as she pushed open the doors into the President's office. Her husband always had the answers to whatever troubles the colony had faced. She missed his swift mind and sure hand.

Katrina shook her head as memories of their many years together flooded in. She recalled more than a few times when Markus, too, had been frustrated and uncertain.

OK, maybe not all the answers, Katrina thought with a smile on her lips. *But you always had me, and Tanis, and so many of our friends that came with us from Sirius. But they are all gone now. I feel that I have nothing in common with this generation.*

"Katrina!" President Leanne said as she rose from her desk and walked around, holding out her hands for an embrace.

Katrina pulled her mind back into the world around her as she approached Leanne. "Good afternoon, President Leanne," Katrina said before accepting the hug.

"Katrina, please, call me Leanne," the current Victorian President said as they separated. "You spent more time behind this desk than I have—and in more troubled times, too, I might add."

"Thank you, Leanne," Katrina said as she inclined her head and sat in one of the chairs in front of the desk.

She knew it was rude to sit first in a formal setting such as this, but if the years of service she had given weren't enough to let her sit when she was tired, then she didn't know what could possibly earn such leniency.

Leanne didn't react to Katrina's informality as she leaned against her desk.

Perhaps no one cares about our old ways anymore.

The president certainly didn't dress as her forbearers; there was no reason to expect that she would honor their traditions.

Katrina wondered what Markus would think of the president's tight, single-piece outfit, complete with flashing and swirling colors. It would have fit in perfectly in Luminescent Society in the Sirius System—at least Leanne was far too tall to ever pass as a Lumin.

It amazed her that now, four generations later, the people of the Kapteyn Primacy were emulating the very culture that had enslaved their ancestors. A culture that had launched more than one assault on the Kapteyn's Star System.

And they wonder why I want to leave…

"To what do I owe the pleasure of this visit?" Leanne asked, her brilliant green eyes glinting above her smiling blue lips.

"I think you know," Katrina said. "I want a ship. I'm going after the *Intrepid*."

Leanne sighed and ran a hand through her sparkling white hair.

"You were already denied a ship by the Primacy Parliament. What makes you think that I can grant you one?" Leanne asked.

"Because I own it," Katrina replied as she leaned back in her chair. "The *Victory*. It is my ship. I didn't want to have to do this, but I will if you force me."

"What?" Leanne asked. "The *Victory* is an active vessel in the Victorian Space Force. It's not *your* ship."

"You'll find, Governor, that it *is* my ship. If you look at the records, you'll find that Captain Jason Andrews of the ISS *Intrepid* gifted that ship to me personally, to use should I ever wish to journey to New Eden. At the time, I could not imagine leaving the colony that my husband and I spent so long building…but things are different now."

"Huh," Leanne grunted as her eyes darted across records only she could see. "I was not aware of this; it was over thirty years ago."

Katrina nodded. "And the lease renews every five years. I have allowed it to do so in the past, but not this time. I thought that I would give you a heads-up before I reach out to the Secretary of Defense."

"But it's a five-hundred-meter warship!" Leanne exclaimed. "You don't need a ship like that to chase after the *Intrepid*. You just need an interstellar pinnace."

A sardonic smile teased the corners of Katrina's lips. "Yes, that is the point I've been trying to make for some time now, but no one has been listening to me."

Leanne pushed off from the desk and walked to the office's window, staring out for a moment before turning back to look at Katrina. "You're really serious about this? About going after the *Intrepid*?"

"I am." Katrina's voice was unwavering and resolute. "What continues to amaze me is that I'm the only one."

"Everyone is worried about them," Leanne said. "But the government has debated this, and the arguments have all been made. The veil of secrecy is not to be lifted."

"Well, given that it is my ship, it's not the government's call," Katrina replied.

"I don't know that it is yours either. You may get the *Victory* back from the space force, but that doesn't mean that you will be allowed to leave the heliosphere in it," Leanne said as she sat behind her desk, the clear plas surface doing little to mute her clothing's light show.

"The Veil Act is intended to disallow interstellar and trade activities that would reveal that the Kapteyn's Star System is inhabited," Katrina said, trying not to grip the chair's arms. "Flying after the *Intrepid* does not go against the spirit of that act. I should know—I'm one of the signatories on it, for light's sake."

Leanne folded her hands and rested her chin on them. "It may be that the courts will have to decide upon the law's intent, in that regard."

"And the *Victory*?" Katrina asked. "Are you going to fight me on that, as well?"

Leanne sighed. "It's a warship, it crews over four hundred. You have no need of such a vessel."

"Are you sure that is how you want to play this?" Katrina asked. "I know our laws very well."

"Katrina, this will drag on for years," Leanne said, her tone moving into the realm of conciliatory pleading. "In the end, you'll lose."

Katrina rose from her seat. "I've given you fair warning of what I intended to do. This is a thing that will happen. Even if

I have to regain the Victorian Presidency, or become the Primacy's Chancellor."

Leanne's eyes grew wide. "Katrina—"

"I'll be seeing you," Katrina said and turned away. A smile formed on her lips as she walked out of the president's office.

Leanne called out to her one last time, but Katrina ignored it.

<Think she bought it?> Katrina asked.

<I almost bought it,> Troy replied. *<You're very convincing…in a strange, understated sort of way.>*

<It's an art,> Katrina replied as she walked across the president's outer room toward the lift. *<Don't belabor your point, don't make it seem like there's a way they can wiggle in.>*

<She's already filed an injunction against you taking back the Victory,*>* Troy said. *<Not wasting any time.>*

Katrina smiled as she stepped into the lift. *<File the paperwork declaring my intent to run for the chancellorship, Troy. If you would be so kind.>*

Troy chuckled before responding. *<Already done. It's as though these people don't know who you are.>*

Katrina leaned against the lift's rear wall. *<That's because they* ***don't****. I was raised by a man who incinerated people on the spot for imagined threats. I double-crossed my own government and fomented rebellion. Everyone who remembers those times, what we had to do… they're gone—I am the last.>*

SUITE WITH A VIEW

STELLAR DATE: 08.20.4330 (Adjusted Gregorian)
LOCATION: Katrina's Quarters, High Victoria
REGION: Victoria, Kapteyn Primacy, Kapteyn's Star System

"They're watching your suites, you know," Laura said as she sat on a sofa in Katrina's lounge.

Katrina poured two glasses of white wine—Laura's favorite—and turned toward the seating area. "I know. Troy has it all in hand. Right now, I have no need to deceive; subterfuge will come later."

"The nets are ablaze with the rumors of what a run for Chancellor by the Matrem Katrina could mean," Laura said as she took the glass of wine from Katrina. "And speculation about the real reasons why you're doing this is beginning to circulate."

Katrina sat and nodded silently, staring out the wraparound window that nearly encircled the entire lounge. It provided a brilliant view of several levels of High Victoria 'below' them on the ring, and beyond, the world of Victoria below.

"Are you not worried?" Laura asked.

Katrina glanced at her friend and smiled. Laura was a young woman, only thirty-five years old. She hadn't been born yet when President Tom had attempted to kidnap Tanis and the *Intrepid*'s command crew; neither had she seen the Sirian fleet dissolve into atoms as the Edener's picotech obliterated ships and crews alike.

Laura had never fought the fires that burned across the surface of Victoria after the wreckage fell, attended the hundreds of funerals, or testified at the mass trials where the Sirian invaders were given lifelong prison sentences—those who were spared the death penalty, anyway.

To her, that was a history lesson—even the *Intrepid*'s departure was a dim childhood memory to her.

Yet somehow, Laura understood Katrina better than anyone.

"Worried?" Katrina repeated the question. "No. Evaluating, yes. Well, I am worried. But it's for you, Laura. I should fire you soon. When my plan comes to fruition, your part in it will not be looked upon kindly."

Laura shrugged. "I've done nothing illegal…at least not that anyone can trace back to me—I hope."

<*You're safe,*> Troy said on the suite's local net. <*There are so few AIs in this system, it is a simple task to ensure that the records reflect what we want them to.*>

"Helps that all the AIs here revere you as a hero and a miracle, Troy," Katrina said.

<*I think it's* **you** *that they revere,*> Troy replied.

Katrina laughed and shook her head. She was the one who had spearheaded the mission to find AIs lost in the Battle for Victoria. The planet's moon, Anne, had been riddled with so much debris coming down over the years, that many had said it was a fool's errand; yet the intact cores of both Troy and Jerome had been found on Anne's surface.

It was a rescue operation that had earned Katrina the gratitude of the remaining AIs in The Kap.

Troy's AI core now rested in a pillar in the center of the sitting room—where he'd remained since being restored after the rescue. Katrina gazed at it for a moment as she held her glass to her lips.

"Command calling Kat." Laura gave a small wave. "You still with us?"

"Hmmm?" Katrina said, focusing on Laura. "Yes, sorry, I was just letting my mind wander for a minute. Are you sure you don't want to come with us?"

Laura shook her head. "Yes…no…I wish I could, Kat. They're important to you, the Edeners. And your friend, Tanis—she means the world to you, and you miss her greatly. I can see it in your eyes whenever you think about where that ship might be. I—"

Katrina reached out and touched Laura's hand as she saw tears from in her friend's eyes. "You fear you'll feel the same way about me when I'm gone."

Laura nodded wordlessly and turned her face aside.

"It's OK for you to feel torn about this," Katrina said softly. "These things are never easy. The heart cannot decide, so the mind must. I let my mind keep me here; held in place by my duty, my dedication. But my heart is stronger now…and the stars call me."

Laura turned to face Katrina, tears spilling out of her eyes once more. "Will you ever come back, Kat?"

"'Ever'…. Ever is a long, long time, Laura. But I do not know, and I do not wish to sow false hope in you."

Neither woman spoke for several minutes. Katrina's hips began to feel stiff. She stretched and let out a long sigh. "I feel like I'm betraying him."

"By leaving?" Laura asked. "From what you've told me, I think he'd care that you were happy more than anything."

Katrina nodded. "That I understand. I meant the rejuvination. I grew old with him out of respect—stayed old for the same reason. I've become accustomed to being an old woman. I think it suits me—but in a couple weeks, I undo that. It feels like erasing our time together."

"He'll be forever in your heart, just like a piece of mine is with you, Kat," Laura whispered. "A part of it will travel across the stars with you, and be lost to me forever. But should I go with you, I'd feel the same loss for my family."

Katrina gave Laura a kindly smile. "There is no need to be so fatalistic about it. The heart will heal."

"Yours hasn't," Laura said quietly.

"Yes," Katrina said with a nod. "But mine, I think, has suffered more than most."

*****

Katrina stared at the holoprojection of herself, and gave a tentative smile. She felt like she was seeing a ghost, a vision from the past.

She was young again.

The rejuv treatment had taken over a week, the doctor admonishing her many times about how long she had let herself go. Over the years, her bone density had decreased and her muscles had weakened. The deterioration had required the regrowth of much of her skeleton, and reinforcement of her joints and ligaments.

Many of her upgrades from the days before she had joined the Noctus rebellion in the Sirius System had also needed replacing, which was fine by Katrina. She would rather be augmented by Edener tech than that of her former people any day.

The doctor had also found it necessary to completely regrow her skin, as well as replace her eyes, which had suffered too much cone and rod damage over the decades to repair.

The process had begun to take so long that she worried it would require postponing her plans, but in the end, the doctor had finished with a day to spare.

She had made one tweak after the doctor's work was done. She had used her nano to create small crow's feet around her eyes. A reminder that though she appeared to be a young woman, she was not. Not in her heart.

As she turned and examined her features, the memories that came over her were bittersweet. She hadn't looked like this since the rebellion on the *Hyperion*. Since before the fifty-year journey to Kapteyn's Star.

Since she and Markus had been young and falling in love.

"Oh, Markus, you stubborn old man; why did you have to leave me?" Katrina whispered softly.

<*Does it ever hurt less?*> Troy asked, his tone sympathetic—a rarity for him.

Katrina shook her head. "No, though I think of him less as time goes on…only a thousand times a day instead of ten thousand." She gave a self-deprecating laugh. "Does it feel like that for you, Troy? AIs love, in their own way, don't they? You had loved ones on the *Intrepid*."

<*It is different,*> Troy replied. <*AIs in general are very good at compartmentalizing; I'm probably better than most. I know it sounds silly, but I think I miss Tanis more than anyone else. Except for Bob, but I miss what he is, as much as himself.*>

"Tanis…the cure for all our woes," Katrina whispered with a shake of her head.

<*We should not place so much hope in her,*> Troy said. <*We must find that within ourselves; another cannot complete you.*>

"I know that, Troy. Sometimes, though…sometimes I feel like the well is dry."

<*Forgive me for speaking so bluntly, Katrina, but you need to get out of your own head. We're going to be alone for some time in the black. I can't be your psychiatrist for the trip. If you can't keep yourself from wallowing in despair, I won't do this.*>

Troy's words stung, but she knew he was right. If she spent the next decade pining and yearning for everything she no longer had, she would destroy herself.

Something that would be all too easy out in the black.

Katrina narrowed her eyes, watching the holoprojection follow suit. "You're right, Troy. As you so often are, you bitter old thing. I still have steel in me, and I know we'll find the

Intrepid. They're out there, and sure as the stars burn, we will find them."

<That's the spirit, Katrina.>

She stooped over and grabbed the bag that held personal mementos from her years at The Kap, while the case containing her clothing and other personal necessities rolled across the bedroom toward her.

As she straightened, Katrina smiled at how nice it felt not to have her bones creak in protest. She surveyed her room; the bed was not perfectly made, there was a dress draped over a chair, the bathroom light was on.

It was the room of someone who planned to return soon, not someone who would never come back.

She walked out into her suite's living room and approached Troy's column.

<Your pinnace is fueled and ready,> Troy said. *<I've altered the dock records to show a fuel level suitable for the trip to Tara.>*

"What would I do without you, Troy?" Katrina asked as she stood in front of his column.

<Remain trapped here in the Kapteyn's Star System, I suspect,> Troy paused, and Katrina took the opportunity to give a soft laugh before the AI continued. *<I'm ready. Yank me.>*

The column's light blue glow faded, and a panel slid aside. Within lay the tetrahedron-like cube that was Troy's core. She reached in and carefully lifted it from the data socket, then slipped it into a protective case on the coffee table.

The case had both power and wireless Link access, and once the core settled into the socket, Troy's voice came back to her.

<Guh, I hate how that feels. It's like knowing that someone can transplant your brain in seconds—well, not 'like' that, it **is** *that.>*

"Sorry, can't really take your column."

<Don't worry,> Troy replied. *<I'm eager to finally get back in a ship. I should have done it sooner…>*

"There are a lot of things we both should have done sooner," Katrina replied. "OK, here goes."

She placed Troy's protective case on top of the rolling case containing her clothing, and pulled a strap over both. Once satisfied that Troy was secure, Katrina walked to her suite's door.

As it slid open, she came face to face with Laura.

"Katrina!" Laura exclaimed. "I've been trying to reach you, but you haven't responded to my calls and your suite denied me access…"

"Yes, Laura," Katrina replied evenly. "I've decided to let you go. I no longer require your services."

The look of pain that flooded Laura's features was so genuine that Katrina knew she was drawing on real sorrow. Good, the girl had potential.

"But…Katrina, I was to come with you to Tara! You're going to need help interviewing the campaign manager positions. I…I don't understand."

"Laura," Katrina said, her tone not entirely unkind. "We talked about this. I need someone who has experience in politics to be my personal assistant. You have potential, but this run is too important for me to mentor you along the way. I really am sorry, but our time together is over."

Laura's face fell and Katrina wanted to reach out to the young woman, to tell her that she was a dear friend, and to remind her that these words were an act.

But she could not. After Katrina did what she planned, Laura's life would be under a microscope. This conversation would be pulled from the passageway's cameras, and if it was discovered that Katrina had spoken with Laura over the Link while dismissing her aloud, it would destroy the credibility of the scene.

"When you come back from Tara?" Laura asked, her voice wavering, "I can resume my service, then? I just want to work with you, Katrina; to be the personal assistant of the chancellor would be amazing, and I want to be by your side."

Katrina peered into Laura's eyes and saw no lie in those words. She knew that Laura felt more than a professional affection for her—but for Katrina, it was motherly…or maybe grandmotherly. It was one of the reasons she was glad that Laura had decided of her own accord to stay behind.

There was no small risk in this journey, and risk would be too hard to undertake with this wonderful woman at her side.

And there was also Markus.

Markus still had too much of her heart to share the remainder with someone else. It would not be fair.

"No, Laura. Your service to me is over. Now if you'll excuse me, I must be on my way. I have departure checks to perform."

The coldness in her voice hurt both women, and Laura clutched at her arm. "No, Katrina, please, please let me come with you. This can't be the end."

Katrina shook Laura's hand free. "Laura. Pull yourself together. You are a smart woman with a bright future ahead of you. It is with a heavy heart that I terminate your employment with me. But my recommendation for you is on record. Take that, and retain your dignity. Now allow me to be on my way in peace."

She spoke the last word with a ringing finality and watched a tear slip down Laura's face.

"Goodbye," Katrina said, and turned away. The sight of Laura's pained expression would become another memory in a long list that would haunt her forever.

Katrina knew at the end, as she'd pleaded, Laura had not been acting.

DEPARTURE

STELLAR DATE: 08.20.4330 (Adjusted Gregorian)
LOCATION: Bay 148, Docking Ring 4, High Victoria
REGION: Victoria, Kapteyn Primacy, Kapteyn's Star System

Half an hour later, as Katrina settled into the cockpit of her pinnace, she let the tears come. Not just for Laura and the way they had parted—even though it was out of necessity—but also because she would never set foot in High Victoria again.

The suite that she had left in moderate disarray was where she had spent her final years with Markus. It was where so much good time had been spent.

"It'll be good to leave," Katrina said. "Too many memories here. I need to stop living in the past."

Even as she said it, Katrina knew that a wild chase after the *Intrepid* was not so very different. She was desperately pursuing the past; eager to relive those golden years while the Victoria colony was being built. The years of working late with Markus, and counselling both he and Tanis on how the integration of the Victorians and the Edeners should best proceed.

She hoped that Laura would carry on that legacy. The woman had a bright future, and she had a good heart. When she got the message that Katrina had left for her, perhaps she would be able to do what Katrina could not.

Katrina took a deep breath and opened Troy's protective case.

"Here goes," she said.

<*Just get it over with,*> the AI replied.

A chuckle followed by a sniff escaped her, and she wiped her eyes, drying her hands on her pants. Katrina pulled Troy's core from the case's socket, and placed it on the pedestal between the two seats in the pinnace's small cockpit.

Once securely in place, the pedestal retracted into the floor, taking Troy's core with it.

<*Why, oh, why did I wait so long?*> Troy asked. <*I'd almost forgotten what it is like to have a body.*>

"Bodies are nice," Katrina said. "Though I've never gone without one, so it's just an assumption that they're preferable."

<*Trust me,*> Troy replied. <*Much more preferable.*>

"Dockmaster has us cleared," Katrina said. "Should be transferring to the launch rail in three minutes."

<*Confirmed,*> Troy said. <*Perry will have us out in the black, and then we can finally get this show on the road.*>

Once in space, the pair would pilot the pinnace in a slingshot around Victoria, which would line them up on the proper trajectory for Tara—the second terraformed world in the Kapteyn's Star System.

Tara, a moon of Albion—the third planet in the Kapteyn's Star System—was smaller than Victoria. Though Tara was a pleasant world with less than 1*g* of gravity, its parent planet, Albion, was a massive super-earth with a punishing 5*g*s of gravity.

With other planets and asteroids offering much more easily-accessible resources in the Kap's System, the surface of Albion was relatively untouched. A few mining outposts—mostly automated—dotted its surface where exotic elements had been found over the years.

It was to one of those mining outposts—not the world of Tara—that Katrina and Troy were headed; or so the Primacy Space Force would ultimately believe.

A request reached the edge of Katrina's mind, and she saw that it was President Leanne. She let out a long-suffering sigh and accepted the communication.

<*Katrina, I understand that you're departing for Tara today,*> Leanne said without greeting.

<*I am,*> Katrina replied.

<*To interview candidates for your staff, I understand?*> Leanne asked.

<*Yes, I am going to start with the outer worlds and habitats, and work my way back in to Victoria. I should have a full staff for my run in just a few months.*>

That much was true. Katrina had booked meetings with hundreds of individuals, both humans and AIs; all lined up to fill various roles in her campaign. It was not the first time she had run for office; anyone looking over her itinerary would have no reason to doubt that she was engaged in the opening stages of a major political run.

Katrina wasn't running for Leanne's job, but that of the Chancellorship. Therefore, theoretically, Leanne shouldn't care; but ever since Katrina had declared her intent to run, she had seen how the Victorian president carried more than a little water for the chancellor.

<*I really wish you'd drop this,*> Leanne said. <*We know why you're running for office. It's a ridiculous rationale, and one that Chancellor Shelly will not hesitate to drag out into the light. You can't run for office just to get your way when it comes to finding the* Intrepid.>

<*That's where you're wrong,*> Katrina replied. <*I can run on whatever platform I want. That's why we have a democracy. Will Shelly defeat me at the polls? Maybe. But she got into office on my endorsements in the first place. Now she'll drag me through the mud—the last living member of the* Hyperion's *exodus from Sirius—just to win? It will damage her as much as me.*>

Leanne took a moment to respond, and Katrina knew that she had hit upon the heart of the matter. Beating Katrina at the polls would require discrediting her thoroughly. But that was a dangerous thing to do. It could backfire and be perceived as a hate campaign by the public.

Finally, Leanne spoke. *<You leave me no choice. I'm calling the dockmaster; your flight privileges are revoked, and you will be put under house arrest for taking actions against the Veil Act.>*

Katrina allowed a laugh to pass across the Link to Leanne. *<That's your play? Lock me up in my tower so that I cannot cause you any problems?>*

<Your goal is to break the law,> Leanne said.

<Well, she has that right,> Troy said privately, listening in on the conversation.

Katrina didn't respond to Troy. He was right, but Leanne was doing this to stop legal democratic change; the thought that she would abuse her power like this incensed Katrina. However, anger would not serve her, so she pushed those feelings down and replied calmly. *<I plan to change the law, legally. Besides, Leanne—you may be the President of Victoria, but there is nothing you can do to stop me. Goodbye.>*

Katrina closed the connection and looked at the countdown on the holodisplay. Just over a minute until the pinnace moved to the launch rail.

A message came through on the docking bay's net, and Katrina switched it to audible systems.

It was Perry, High Victoria's dockmaster. "You certainly pissed someone off, Katrina."

"Well, people don't want to know what will happen if I get back in power. There'd be some house cleaning, to be sure."

"Oh, I don't doubt it," Perry said with his deep chuckle. "Oh, wow, they've put President Leanne on; she really wants me to stop your launch."

"I assume you have a contingency?" Katrina asked evenly. She was placing a lot of faith in Perry. He was a good man, and she remembered bouncing him on her knee when he was a baby. She hated to call in such a big favor from him, but given that it was her last, she hoped he wouldn't mind.

"Oh, yeah," Perry said, his words dripping out in a droll tone. "The cradle your pinnace is on was due for maintenance a few weeks back, but no one got to it. Now we can't stop it from launching without doing a full system reset, and...well, that takes ten minutes."

"Thanks, Perry," Katrina said.

"Thank you, Katrina," the dockmaster replied. "My gran always said that none of us would be here—that our grandparents and great grandparents would have all died back in Sirius—if not for you. Making sure you get to take your bird out seems like a pathetic repayment by comparison."

"Nevertheless, thank you."

The pinnace vibrated as the cradle slipped over the rail launch system. The ship's holodisplay lit up with the launch control countdown.

"Happy flying, Matrem Katrina. See you when you get back."

"You bet," Katrina lied. "When I get back—maybe then you'll have this cradle fixed."

Perry laughed. "Maybe I will."

The dockmaster signed off and, a moment later, the cradle dropped into the deck, settling the pinnace onto the launch rail. A clang reverberated through the ship, and then the rail grabbed hold and pulled the small craft forward out of the docking bay, accelerating it down a long chute.

And then they were in space.

Katrina ran a systems check, though it was just a perfunctory review of Troy's work. Everything looked good.

<*We're in the pocket for the slingshot maneuver,*> Troy said. <*STC has denied our flight path, but it's still clear of traffic.*>

"They're really pulling out the stops here," Katrina said. "If I were actually running for office, I would crucify them for all of this."

<*They must suspect that you're up to something,*> Troy said. <*This isn't a rational response from them otherwise.*>

"Or they're taking advantage of my stubbornness to make a criminal out of me," Katrina replied, her voice far calmer than she felt.

<*Burning now,*> Troy announced.

The pinnace boosted around Victoria in a broad arc, angling to remain close to the planet as the engines pushed the small ship to a far greater velocity than required for breakaway.

The roar of the chemical burn taking place only twenty meters away thrummed through her body, and Katrina closed her eyes, clamping her jaw shut as the pinnace skipped across the upper levels of Victoria's atmosphere.

When their trajectory lined up with Tara, Troy rotated the ship, punched the boosters once more, and the vessel broke free from Victoria's ionosphere, shooting out toward the distant world.

Katrina opened her eyes as the boost evened out and the ship ceased shaking. Then the chemical thrusters cut off, and the fusion engine activated. The burn was low, just a trickle, but the fusion drive delivered over 2*g* of continuous thrust, driving the ship ever onward.

"Oh, great," Katrina said as scan lit up with the signature of a cruiser closing in on them. "Leanne's really lost it, now."

<*You make it sound like we didn't plan for this,*> Troy said.

"Well, yeah, I know we did, but that still doesn't make me happy that it's happening," Katrina replied.

<*They're hailing us,*> Troy said.

"You can actually pick that one hail out from everyone trying to contact us right now? Even half the news agencies are trying to reach me for a statement. I've had to queue all incoming connections."

<*Child's play, Katrina. Want me to put it on?*>

"Yeah, they have to get closer before we can deal with them, anyway. A little chat will be a good distraction."

<*For them or for us?*>

"Both, I suppose."

As Katrina had planned, the cruiser that the Primacy Space Force was putting in her path was her ship, the *Victory*. She also knew who the captain was—a man named Wilson, who was less than pleased that Katrina wanted to take his command away.

"Matrem Katrina," he said, his posture stiff and formal when he appeared on the holo. "You will cease burn and prepare to dock with the *Victory*. You are to be taken into custody for violations against the Veil Act."

"Captain Wilson," Katrina replied with a sweet smile. "It's so good to see you. I trust you're taking care of my ship? No scuffs or scratches?"

"I heard of your plan to end our lease of the *Victory*," Captain Wilson said with a deep frown. "Not that anything will come of it—especially now that you've committed acts of treason."

Katrina laughed. "Seriously, Captain. What acts of treason? I am a free citizen, flying my stellar pinnace. This ship couldn't even make it to the heliopause, let alone out into interstellar space. What Veil Act violation have I made?"

"That doesn't matter," Wilson replied as he pulled himself up straight, his expression somehow both magnanimous and haughty. "I have my orders. You will dock with this ship and be taken into custody."

"Which ship?" Katrina asked with a smirk.

Wilson's brow furrowed. "The *Victory*, my ship."

"We've been over this, Captain Wilson. The *Victory* is *my* ship." As she spoke, Katrina sent the command override codes, which the space force did not know she had.

For a moment, nothing happened, and she worried that the space force had discovered the alterations she had made long ago, before leasing the ship to them.

Captain Wilson began to speak again; something about a timeline, and cooperation being encouraged. Katrina muted him.

<*Don't worry, they won't have found what you did. It was masterfully done,*> Troy said, his mental tone filled with confidence. <*These chuckleheads won't know what happened to them.*>

<*They may be chuckleheads, but they're not rank amateurs,*> Katrina replied.

<*And there the* Victory *goes,*> Troy said with a laugh. <*Care to reassess their skill level?*>

Sure enough, the *Victory* suddenly changed course and began a hard burn away from the pinnace. Katrina saw a look of anger and consternation cross Captain Wilson's face before the *Victory*'s comm systems shut down.

"I sure wish they had been reasonable," Katrina said. "A ship like the *Victory* would have been much better than what we'll have to make do with."

<*Yeah, but there're just too many people on it,*> Troy said. <*We could get them off, but someone would get hurt, and then you'd go down in history as the woman who killed the crew of a ship as she fled the system.*>

"Seems a bit melodramatic," Katrina said.

<*What can I say?*> Troy replied. <*I'm all about the hyperbole.*>

Katrina snorted a laugh and then scowled at the console. "I see what you're doing. No cheering me up. I'm supposed to be sad and melancholy as we flee the system."

<*Sure, insist on it; the airlock's just over there. Go mope in space,*> Troy winked in Katrina's mind.

"Ass," Katrina laughed. It was a real laugh. As it left her lips, she felt as though something was lifting off her; a malaise that had hung over her heart ever since the day the *Intrepid* had failed to send its update.

The cloud of worry wasn't gone, just less ominous now that she had a plan of action and was executing it.

She would see this through.

Scan showed a dozen patrol ships boosting toward the pinnace, and Katrina checked and rechecked their vector.

"We're in the pocket," she said. "Passing behind Anne in fifteen minutes. Well ahead of any of their intercept times."

<Yup; helps to have accomplices in every corner.>

Katrina couldn't agree more. This escape would never have worked without just about every AI in the system aiding them. From ensuring that the *Victory* was the ship closest when they broke orbit form Victoria, to altering schedules and patrol patterns across the system. Katrina would be forever indebted to the AIs of The Kap.

Neither she nor Troy spoke as the pinnace raced toward Anne, and the blind spot in the system scan that had been created by the aforementioned AIs.

Once the pinnace passed behind the moon, Katrina activated the ship's stealth systems, while Troy gave a small burn to nudge the ship onto a new trajectory.

They weren't completely invisible; it wasn't as though the pinnace had anything approaching the *Andromeda*'s stealth tech. But the ship was small, and so long as no one was looking for them along this new trajectory, they would slip by unseen.

Or so she hoped.

PERSEUS

STELLAR DATE: 08.29.4330 (Adjusted Gregorian)
LOCATION: *Voyager*, Approaching Perseus
REGION: Kapteyn Primacy, Kapteyn's Star System

Perseus was interdicted.

Even though Tanis had seen every trace of the secret picotech research facility—known as the Gamma Site—destroyed, the dwarf planet was still off limits.

Fortunately for Katrina and Troy, few Victorians had any desire to travel to Perseus. Few things were more terrifying than the vids of the Edener picobombs obliterating the remains of the Sirian fleet in minutes. The thought of encountering, or unleashing, some hidden cache of pico on Perseus was more than enough to keep most people away.

Still, there were always those with an insatiable curiosity, and the Primacy Space Force kept a patrol craft in orbit, along with a sensor web.

<Damn, we're not lined up properly,> Troy said as they approached the dwarf world.

"I was afraid of that. We made it here a touch too fast."

<It also looks like Jerome initiated the maintenance routines a bit too soon; the dead zone is way out of alignment.>

Katrina examined the sensor net around Perseus. They were close to the edge of the disabled section in the sensor net. It was possible that they could make it through undetected.

"I say we give the tiniest burn to nudge ahead, and then go for the hole," Katrina said.

<That'll light us up,> Troy replied. *<There's no way to hide that, the entire system is searching for us right now.>*

"Yeah, but it will take half a day for the light from the burn to make it to the closest pursuer. If we can angle the ship enough to hide our burn from the patrol craft, we should be OK."

Troy didn't respond immediately, and Katrina was glad that he didn't dismiss her plan out of hand.

<OK, let's do it. If we don't, we'll pass right through the active web anyway, and there's no way we can hide from active scan at that range.>

"Glad you agree," Katrina replied.

<Agree is a strong word. It's more like 'can't be any worse'.>

"Gee, thanks for the ringing endorsement."

The nav holo updated with the burn location and the new trajectory. It would put them a thousand kilometers inside the sensor net's dead zone, and their wash would be pointed away from the patrol ship, but that ship would only be ten thousand kilometers distant. If it spotted them, they'd be well within its weapons range.

The space force wasn't quite at the point of 'shoot first, ask questions later', but they certainly weren't happy about the million kilometer burn Katrina had sent the *Victory* on.

When the time for the brief burn came, it was anticlimactic—just a twenty-second boost followed by an hour-long drift toward Perseus. Then Troy spun the ship and began a slow burn with the engines pointed at the dwarf world's surface.

"So far so good," Katrina said as they closed to within one thousand kilometers of the planet.

<Seems so. The patrol craft hasn't altered its trajectory.>

"Most of the space force's attention appears to be on Tara and Albion. I bet our friendly neighborhood patrol boat is looking that way, too."

<Let's hope,> Troy said.

Although Tanis had burned away the Gamma Site picotech research facility—with plasma, no less—there was a secondary site on Perseus. It was an emergency evac location for the

Gamma Site scientists. Few knew of its location and, other than herself and Troy, none of those people were within a light year of The Kap.

<Once again sneaking onto Perseus,> Troy said as they continued to descend toward the barren surface of the planet.

"That's right, you've been here before," Katrina said.

<Several times,> Troy said. *<The first was back when we delivered the picotech to the facility.>*

"With Tanis and Joe," Katrina said. "Wasn't that right before the attempted assassination at the city hall on Landfall?"

<Yup, it was,> Troy replied. *<That was one hell of an escape you guys pulled that day, by the way.>*

Katrina nodded silently. "It was mostly Tanis. I still can't believe her pain tolerance; she melted the skin off her hands sealing those rocks."

<I can only imagine what that's like. Angela showed me the images—it certainly didn't look pleasant.>

"In better news, looks like we're lined up right on top of the evac site."

<Yup, touching down in fifteen. Why don't you get suited up? You'll have to go across the surface to get in there.>

"You got it," Katrina said. "We're almost home free."

<We're still a long way from interstellar space, Katrina.>

"Killjoy."

*****

The pinnace settled down on the dwarf world's hard regolith; nothing more than a small speck in the shadow of a deep crater on the planet's night side.

It had taken no small amount of work to align so many variables; the patrol routes, the personnel shifts, the orbits of the worlds—but so far, everything was going according to plan.

Katrina expected that to end at any moment.

She rechecked the seals on her EVA suit one more time before palming the control to open the pinnace's hatch. The small craft had no airlock, and the air was slowly drawn out of the ship until there was vacuum within as well as without.

Once the interior pressure reached zero, the hatch opened and Katrina stepped out, turning to grab her bag and the two cases: one containing her clothing, and the other containing Troy.

<*The indignities we must suffer,*> Troy muttered as Katrina strapped his case to the one containing her clothing, and then slung her duffel over her shoulder. Once satisfied that everything was secure, she hefted the cases and began to take slow, loping steps.

<*Hush, no EM,*> Katrina replied.

<*It's narrowband, it won't make it more than a hundred meters,*> Troy countered.

Katrina sighed. AIs without all their memory cores powered on were annoyingly forgetful.

<*This place is not without its defenses,*> Katrina said <*Now hush 'til I put you in the next ship.*>

If it was still there.

This entire mission hinged on a gamble: that Tanis hadn't taken the evac ship from the Gamma Site.

Katrina had scoured the records of the site's cleanup and the shutdown of the mining operations on Perseus. Nothing showed the ship being extracted. Logic would dictate, then, that the vessel was still there—but Tanis was not known for missing things.

Which was why Katrina worried.

What will we do if there's no ship? Katrina asked herself for the hundredth time since leaving her suite on High Victoria.

In truth, she did not know. A part of her was determined to take the pinnace into interstellar space; though it did not have the shielding nor the fuel supplies to make that a safe endeavor.

The only course of action with the pinnace was to point the ship at New Eden and pray that the stasis chamber would last the hundreds of years it would take to cross between the star systems.

She couldn't shake the feeling that such a course of action was akin to suicide. But remaining at The Kap—even if she wasn't imprisoned—would be another sort of suicide. No matter what the risk, Katrina preferred a future of her own making over all else.

It was why she had joined the Lumins' spy agency in Sirius. It had been an act of rebellion against her father, though he had ultimately managed to move her under his purview anyway.

I should have left with the Intrepid, Katrina thought as she approached the location marked on her HUD as the service entrance to the Gamma Evac Site.

Katrina saw a flash and heard a small explosion to her right. She dropped into a low crouch, looking for adversaries and incoming weapons fire.

None came, and she rose, walking toward the location of the explosion.

Just a meteor.

That was the worst thing about EVA on an airless place like Perseus. Any object caught in the planet's gravitational pull would continue to accelerate until it hit the surface of the world. On planets with atmosphere, incoming objects slowed in the air, fracturing and disintegrating long before reaching the ground.

Here, every pebble falling from space hit with the force of a kinetic weapon, easily enough to tear through Katrina's suit and body.

She quickened her pace, and reached the spot marked as the entrance a minute later.

The surface of the moon held no visible sign that there was anything out of the ordinary, but Katrina's upgraded eyes could see a single rock that had a distinct refractive profile. She reached down and touched it. An EM signal flared from the rock, and Katrina received a response from a previously inactive network.

The network prompted her for authorization codes, and Katrina furnished her personal key, and the token she had used while president.

The network signaled its acceptance, and Katrina breathed a sigh of relief as a section of the crater floor sank, revealing a dark shaft. Katrina peered over the edge and saw a lift rising to the surface.

When it arrived, she set her cases on the platform, stepped on, and pushed the lone button on the lift's control panel.

She took a deep breath as the lift shuddered before beginning to descend. Above, the opening slowly closed, blotting out the night stars gleaming above Perseus.

Katrina wasn't certain if it was poetic or a harbinger of doom, but the last star visible was Sirius.

For a moment, the shaft was dark as the lift soundlessly descended deep beneath the surface of the planet. Then a string of lights came on, and Katrina peered over the railing, gauging the drop to be well over a kilometer.

She shook her head with a grim smile. The Gamma Site apparently had never been visited by a safety inspector; a slip over the low rail, and she'd do an impersonation of the meteor that hit the surface not long ago.

When the lift reached the bottom of the shaft, she pushed her cases into a waiting airlock, and signaled it to cycle.

<*May I speak now, oh Queen of Silence?*> Troy's sardonic tone made her smile at the AI's neverending supply of surliness.

<*So long as you're nice,*> Katrina said with a broad smile on both her face, and that of her net avatar.

<*Like that's ever stopped me before. Wait…why are you so happy? Do you see it in the inventory?*>

<*I didn't look at the inventory, it's on the map.*>

<*Huh, look at that.*>

Katrina brought up the route to the ship's bay and pushed her cases through the halls at a near run. A part of her was wracked with fear that the map was wrong, that there was no ship in the bay—that it would be empty when she arrived.

But it was not.

In the bay, the ship—a two-hundred-meter, interstellar-capable scout interceptor—stood on its engines, mounted to a launch rail, ready to take them into the black.

<*The* Voyager. *That's almost uncanny,*> Troy commented.

Katrina nodded as she brought up the *Voyager*'s readiness report. It was fueled, stocked with food and other supplies, and the SC batteries were fully charged…the ship was ready to go.

<*I can't believe it. I can't freaking believe it…it's here, it's really here!*>

<*Great, now stop talking about it and get me up there. I hate being in this case.*>

Katrina laughed and stepped onto a lift that took her up to the launch bay's catwalks. The lift stopped at the upper catwalk, one hundred and eighty meters above the floor of the bay. She carefully pushed the cases along the steel grating, and then onto the gantry that connected to the ship's waiting airlock.

The overwhelming sense of relief that the ship really was here, that it was right in front of her, was palpable. She almost expected the *Voyager* to be a mirage, a hallucination that would evaporate the moment she reached the airlock.

But it didn't. She stepped into the airlock, and the physical presence of the ship—thankfully—persisted. Once the lock was cycled, Katrina walked onto the ship's fourth level and searched for a convenient place to store her belongings.

The *Voyager* was intended to always be under thrust, either accelerating or braking, so the decks were stacked like floors in a building, with the engines being 'down'.

The level she was on was labeled Deck 3, with only the Ops Deck and Flight Deck above it. Below were four passenger decks, a cargo bay, and a hydroponics and life support deck below that. The bottom deck was the engineering compartment, where the power plant, SC batts, and fusion burners were located.

The antimatter-pion drive was at the very rear of the ship, only accessible from the outside.

Once she had her bag and case carefully stowed, Katrina climbed the central ladder to the Ops Deck where Troy's AI core would be housed.

He powered his core down in preparation, and Katrina keyed in a command sequence on a panel to open the AI core housing. A panel slid open, revealing a socket for the core, and Katrina carefully placed Troy into it.

The panel closed and sealed, and a moment later Troy was back.

<Oh a ship, a real ship. It's so good to be back.>

"I'm glad you feel that way," Katrina said aloud after removing her helmet. "I'm going to climb up to the flight deck and start the checks."

<I have that in hand,> Troy said. *<And the first issue is upon us. We have enough fuel to reach New Eden, but not enough to perform*

an extended search, especially if we want to mirror the Intrepid's *course. We need an additional ten kilos of antimatter, and I'd prefer it if the deuterium were topped off.*>

"Wise words," Katrina replied as she stowed the protective case that had held Troy, and then slid down the ladder back to Deck 3.

The ship's internal pressure was equalized with the base, and Katrina cycled both sides of the airlock open for easier passage—there was no need to wait for the airlock to triple check air pressure each time she went in or out.

Katrina walked across the gantry to the catwalk with a spring in her step, ignoring how empty the launch bay felt with her lone footfalls echoing through it.

It was strange to think that she was the only person on the entire planet. Katrina had been a lot of places, and seen a lot of things, but she had never been the lone human on an entire world before.

"I really am the last woman in the world," she laughed, thinking of all the disaster vids she had seen that touted such a premise.

In a strange way, Perseus *was* a post-apocalyptic world. The only habitations burned away or abandoned, with this one small base remaining as the last functioning facility.

She whistled as the lift lowered to the bay's floor. Once it touched down, she stepped off and walked to the fueling station. There she entered the commands for the umbilicals to extend and top off the deuterium tanks.

With that process underway, Katrina pulled up a map to see where the antimatter storage was—provided there were additional supplies.

Katrina had never personally handled antimatter before; the idea was somewhat terrifying. Ten kilograms of anti-hydrogen was more than enough to obliterate the Evac Site and put a mighty large crack into Perseus.

But Troy was right—she wanted enough fuel to continue the search as long as possible. There was no point in going out just to have to return in a few years.

The map showed a passageway leading off the *Voyager*'s bay to a storage room several hundred meters away. It was marked as possessing antimatter storage systems, but there was no indication as to whether or not any was within.

"Here's hoping," Katrina said as she followed the markers on her map, and she eventually reached a large, sealed door.

It had occurred to her on the walk that if there was still antimatter here, leaving such a substance stored on a forgotten base may not have been the safest move. When the containment vessel finally failed—granted, that would take hundreds or even thousands of years—any antimatter within would come in contact with normal matter. An event that would make for a very bad day if anyone was nearby.

Before opening the door, Katrina queried the Evac Site's systems to get a reading on the antimatter containment. She was relieved to see that it reported full power and 100% containment.

"Well, here goes nothing," she muttered and opened the door.

Inside were five ten-kilogram antimatter cylinders, all standing atop a unit that kept their containment systems powered.

She examined the cylinders and was glad to see that they had onboard superconductor batteries capable of powering their containment fields. The batteries reported a full charge—enough to last a few hours.

<I found five cylinders. Do we have storage for that much?> she asked Troy over the Link.

<I read room for a hundred and fifty kilos in the Voyager's *engine bay. We only have ten right now, so there's plenty of room, bring them all.>*

Katrina sent an affirmative response and grabbed a transport case from a rack on the side of the room. A cart stood next to the door, and she set the case on the cart. Then she opened the case and turned to the first antimatter cylinder. The command to detach it was simple, and Katrina keyed in the instructions, and then twisted the cylinder counterclockwise before pulling it free.

One-by-one she detached each cylinder and set it into a slot in the case. A bead of sweat ran down her face, and she wiped it away. If she never had to handle antimatter again, she would be more than happy.

She placed the fifth cylinder in the case, and then closed it, carefully locking the latch. She looked at the case on the cart and found a strap to wrap around it as well. No need to risk an accidental trip or a bounce in the planet's low gravity sending the case off the cart.

Katrina knew that the chances of anything bad happening were remotely slim, but it *was* antimatter, after all. The energy resting inertly on the cart was greater than that of half a million nuclear bombs.

At least if something goes wrong, I won't even know it.

<*You've got a problem,*> Troy said.

A thousand horrible things raced through Katrina's mind in the time it took her to respond. <*What is it?*>

<*Our friends from the patrol ship must have spotted us. They just blew the surface entrance and are rappelling down the lift shaft.*>

<*That was sneaky of them,*> Katrina replied.

Katrina did some quick math on timing. There was no way she could get the antimatter to the ship before the Primacy Soldiers—she assumed it would be soldiers—made it to the *Voyager*'s bay.

She pulled up the map once more, double-checking the location of the armory she had spotted previously.

It was further from the bay.

She left the cart of antimatter in the storage room and dashed down the hall to the armory, which turned out to be little more than a closet with two powered suits. She shimmied out of her EVA suit and clothing. Once naked, she quickly pulled on a ballistic base layer before backing up to the armor rack. The system activated, and Katrina drew in a deep breath as powered armor folded around her.

A hundred years, at least. That was how long it had been since she'd worn armor. Firing a weapon in anger? That was even further in her past. She dredged up a few mnemonics to help get her ready, and steadied her breathing as the armor system slotted in the additional ablative plating.

<Have they breached the airlock yet?> Katrina asked as she ran through a quick system check on the armor while looking over the weapons selection.

<I put it into a maintenance cycle, and they don't have the codes for this site. I suspect they're gonna blow it. You in EVA?>

<Better. As per usual, Tanis overprepared.>

<Since we always seem to need her over-preparation, do you really think that's what it is.>

Katrina selected a pulse rifle and a multifunction rifle capable of firing both low velocity pellets, and ballistic projectiles.

She didn't want to kill any of the soldiers being sent after her—they were still her people—but she wouldn't be deterred from her course of action. Not when she had made it this far.

She sprinted down the corridor back to the antimatter storage room, the armor's maglock boots allowing her to run at full speed without bounding into the ceiling.

Once inside the room, Katrina unstrapped the antimatter case from the cart and tucked it under her arm.

Carrying fifty kilos would have been a difficult endeavor in just her EVA suit, but the powered armor's actuators made it a breeze. Given that she would be taking fire very shortly—and, by extension, the antimatter case—maneuverability was key.

The ground shook beneath her feet and Katrina knew that her guests had arrived. She pulled up the Evac Site's feeds and saw a dozen Primacy soldiers flood through the airlock. A second later, the base's decompression alarms sounded, and pressure doors began to drop.

<*Shit!*> Katrina swore. <*I wasn't thinking! There are two doors between me and the launch bay.*>

<*You're a little rusty,*> Troy replied. <*I can halt the doors in your section now that the ones near the lock have sealed. Five of their troops have made it through into your part of the base, though. The rest are trying to get through one of the doors that cut them off.*>

Five troops. I can do that. I've faced worse odds in my years.

Katrina deployed the armor's probes and sent them ahead to scout the first of the four intersections between her and the *Voyager*'s bay.

It was clear, and she sent a probe down the cross passage to make sure it stayed that way. The last thing she needed was the enemy flanking her.

The next intersection was clear as well, but the probe she sent down the third corridor stopped responding as soon as it turned the corner.

<*Matrem Katrina! We know you're in here. Come down the corridor, arms up, no weapons.*>

The message was broadcast over the base's public emergency net. After a moment's pause, it began to repeat.

<*How does 'hell no' sound?*> Katrina responded as she checked the map for an alternate route to the launch bay—only to find that there were none.

<*There's no way out, we have your pinnace, you're trapped.*>

<*They don't know about the* Voyager,> Troy said.

<*Yeah, but they must suspect that there's something down here,*> Katrina replied. <*Are they trying to get to the bay?*>

<No, those five are all in the corridor you need to pass.>

Katrina approached the intersection and sent a probe in front of the corridor, getting a view of the five enemies. They were all in cover at another intersection down the cross corridor on the right. Taking them out before they got her would be well-nigh impossible—at least in any reasonable timeframe.

<I'm going to run across this corridor, and I encourage you to go ahead and shoot at me,> Katrina said. *<I'll hold the case of antimatter up nice and high so you can be sure to hit it and kill us all.>*

There was no immediate response, and Katrina took advantage of the distraction to follow through on her promise and dashed across the intersection.

She fired four rounds with the ballistic rifle as she raced by, keeping the shots low. One of the Primacy soldiers fired back, and the shot hit Katrina in the right arm. It was a rail-fired pellet, and the kinetic impact spun Katrina around, slamming her into a wall.

Her arm felt numb and she looked down, half expecting it to be gone, but it was still there—though the armor's ablative plating had been shattered.

She pulled herself back to her feet and took off at top speed, firing behind her as she ran, praying it would be enough to get her to the next pressure door.

Troy must have been watching, because as she approached, the pressure door began to lower.

<Slow it down!> she called out.

<Sorry, the door only has one speed!>

Katrina took her powered armor up to full speed, the maglocks on the boots clacking loudly as they flipped on and off, facilitating her run.

The door was less than half a meter from being fully closed as she slid underneath, pulling the case behind her. A pulse blast hit her side, and she clambered back to her feet as several more shots hit the door and deck.

At least they're not shooting to kill, she thought.

Katrina didn't wait to see how the Primacy soldiers felt about being shut out, and raced down the corridor toward the launch bay. She reached it without incident and boarded the lift, slamming her armored hand into the activation button.

The lift began to rise slowly toward the catwalk, and Katrina looked down to see that the deuterium umbilicals were still connected to the ship.

<Shit, Troy, can you remote detach the fueling line?>

<No, that system is isolated for some reason. You'll need to manually disconnect.>

"Dammit," Katrina swore aloud before setting the antimatter case down and jumping off the lift.

It had only risen thirty meters, and she landed on the deck with a loud *clang!*

The passageway she had just returned through was still empty, and Katrina prayed it would remain so as she ran to the fueling station. The *Voyager*'s tanks were at ninety-five percent, which would have to do.

She keyed in the disconnect command and was about to turn back toward the lift when a shout, amplified by the wearer's armor, called out from behind her.

"Freeze!"

The fueling umbilical disconnected and began to slowly retract as Katrina raised her arms and slowly turned around.

There, at the entrance to the passageway, stood the five Primacy soldiers. Two were standing with their weapons aimed at her, while the other three were carefully moving around the sides of the launch bay to flank her.

Katrina toggled her armor's external speakers and cocked her head before replying. "Why are you doing this? Are you going to kill me for trying to find the *Intrepid*?"

"It doesn't matter," one of the soldiers—a lieutenant, by the marking on his collar—said. "We have our orders. We're to take you into custody."

Katrina took a step toward the lift, which had now reached the top, and lowered her left hand while her right reached behind her back for her multifunction rifle.

"Are you ready to kill me? To go down as the ones who killed the last of the *Hyperion*'s crew? Markus's wife?"

Two of the soldiers flanking her stopped and looked at the lieutenant, though the third kept moving toward her on the left.

"Matrem, don't make us do this," the lieutenant said, and she could hear the anguish in his voice. This man didn't want to be here. He may even agree with her; but she feared that he was honorable, and would do his duty no matter the cost to himself.

<*Thanks for stalling them,*> Troy said privately.

"Oh, you won't do this; you'll only try," Katrina said before diving behind a fuel pump.

Above the soldiers, the *Voyager*'s point defense weapons slid out of the ship's hull and took aim.

"Time to go!" Katrina called out.

The Primacy soldiers didn't move, and Troy opened fire. He didn't target them directly, but the invisible laser beams began to trace glowing lines across the deck toward three of them.

Katrina peered out from behind her cover to see one of the soldiers take aim at the beam's emitter, and she fired a kinetic pellet at him, clipping his arm and spinning him around.

Turnabout is fair play, she thought.

"Fall back!" the lieutenant called out, and Katrina wondered if that was relief she heard in his voice.

She watched four of the soldiers exit the launch bay, and wondered where the fifth had gone. Then she realized the fifth was the one trying to flank her on the left, and spun to see the armored figure come around the other side of the large fuel pump.

A pulse blast hit Katrina center mass, and pushed her back before her boot's maglocks activated.

The soldier, a man by his gait, approached, firing twice more. One shot twisted her sideways, and she let herself fall backward. The second shot rippled through the air above her.

The move had given her time to bring her rifle to bear, and she fired a trio of rounds at the solider—two hitting the man center mass before the rifle's kick sent the third one wide.

The soldier's armor cracked, and he stumbled backward, but he seemed otherwise unharmed.

Katrina didn't wait for him to recover, and flipped to her feet, rushing toward the man, firing twice more with her rifle before she reached him.

The ferocity of her attack appeared to have surprised the Primacy soldier, and she drove a power-assisted fist into his chin, snapping his head back.

He stumbled, and she grabbed the barrel of his weapon and tore it from his grasp, flinging it across the launch bay.

The soldier was undeterred and drew a sidearm. Three shots fired from its muzzle; the first two cracked the armor beneath her rib, and the third penetrated.

Katrina clenched her jaw to keep from screaming, and compressed all the rage and frustration she felt at her own people trying to stop her into cold determination.

If this man wanted a fight to the death, she'd bring it to him.

She took a step to the side to avoid further weapons fire and kicked the soldier's arm, sending his next rounds wide.

Then she lowered her rifle and set it to fire both kinetic and ballistic rounds at the same time—in full automatic.

Katrina fired the weapon over the Link, concentrating on keeping it aimed at the soldier's feet. Three dozen rounds hit the man's feet in three seconds. One of his boots was blown clear off, and the other crumpled under the barrage.

Her goal had only been to disable the maglocks on his boots, but this result would suffice as well. He was screaming in pain as Katrina dropped her rifle, and she scooped the man up—the low gravity and powered armor making it easy.

With a grunt, she tossed him over the fuel pump and toward the entrance where his four teammates had retreated from Troy's laser fire.

"Take him and go!" Katrina called out as she picked up her rifle. She looked down at her side to see biofoam spilling out of her armor and sealing the wound. The bullet was still in there, but that would have to be removed later.

Katrina peered around the pump to see one of the Primacy soldiers dragging her attacker into the passageway. Then her gaze settled on the lift control—which was damaged and sparking.

<*Any chance you can send the lift back down?*> Katrina asked.

<*Nope, another thing in this base that's not on any central control system.*>

Katrina looked for another lift to the catwalk, and spied it across the launch bay. It was no good, though; the soldiers in the passage would have a clear line of sight on her when she reached it.

<*I'm going to climb,*> Katrina said.

<*Better hurry; the rest of their squad has nearly cut through the pressure doors.*>

Katrina slotted the rifle onto her back and ran to the shaft that the lift rode on. She leapt onto it and used the maglocks on her hands and feet to ascend the pole as quickly as she dared.

<*You can't leave!*> The lieutenant's voice called out over the emergency net. <*You're violating the Veil Act.*>

Katrina continued to climb as Troy peppered the entrance to the corridor with laser fire.

<*I don't care.*>

Below, one of the soldiers braved the laser and edged out to take a shot. A projectile ricocheted off Katrina's armor, and Troy responded with a beam that burned the soldier's foot off.

<*I'm as resolute as she is,*> Troy announced to the Primacy soldiers. <*And I'm a lot less sensitive about killing you. This ship is leaving, so I recommend you get out of this base if you don't want it to be filled with your ashes.*>

As he spoke, emergency warning lights began to strobe, and a voice came over the emergency net.

<*Warning, evac ship launching in t-minus five minutes. Rail launch will be assisted by chemical boosters. All personnel, clear the Evac Site.*>

The message repeated as sparks flew from the side of the launching rails, heating the ignition systems for the chemical boosters.

Katrina didn't look to see if the Primacy soldiers were pulling back as she reached the top of the lift's pole. She snatched up the antimatter case as gracefully as she dared, and raced down the catwalk and across the gantry. Once inside the airlock, she slammed her fist into the emergency closure control as the gantry fell away from the ship.

<*What happened to 't-minus five minutes'?*> she asked Troy.

<*Think I'm going to let them know how long they have to shoot us down with their patrol ship?*>

Katrina looked at the case of antimatter and knew she didn't have time to get it into secure storage, so she hauled it up the ladder past the Ops Deck, and onto the Flight Deck.

Unlike the rest of the ship, the cockpit was currently oriented so that the seats faced 'up'. This would give the pilots better support when the ship boosted out into space.

Being pushed back into an acceleration chair was far better than being pushed down into one, something that tended to break spines.

Katrina climbed the rungs built into the floor and slung the case into a seat, buckling the harness around it. Once she was reasonably certain it wouldn't break free, she shimmied into her own seat and buckled in.

The fit was awkward in the powered armor, but she managed to get the harness in place, and pulled up a view of the launch bay on her HUD.

<Looks like they took the hint,> she said when the feeds revealed the soldiers falling back to the entrance shaft.

<It took a few more shots to show them we were serious, but they finally got the message.>

Katrina pulled up the launch status and shook her head. *<Looks like they're trying to stop the launch rails with a remote hack.>*

<Let them try,> Troy said. *<This facility exists for one purpose: to launch this ship. Once that launch is started, it is very, very hard to stop. Plus, I learned a few tricks from Angela during our time together. There's nothing they can do—and even if they could, I'd just fire the fusion engine in here.>*

For the first time, Katrina realized that Troy might be more desperate to leave The Kap than she was.

<Can you really do that? Is it safe?>

Troy chuckled. *<Yes, and not even remotely. Ten seconds, hold on.>*

Katrina switched her view to the top of the launch silo, which was still covered. She was about to say something about it when an explosion flared above, and the doors blew outward.

Then the chemical boosters came alive, and the rail hauled the ship up the kilometer-long shaft, and out into space. The instant they cleared the surface, Troy activated the fusion drives, thrusting the *Voyager* forward at over 10*g*.

Katrina prayed that the Primacy soldiers had not exited the top of the entrance shaft, or it would be the last thing they did.

She didn't have much time to think about it, though. Beams hit the *Voyager*'s hull, and she toggled the refraction shields, limiting the impact of the enemy weaponry.

Enemy. Those were her people. She had worked for decades to build this colony for them; first at her husband's side, and later as governor herself.

Now they were trying to kill her.

She saw the patrol craft sitting in a geostationary orbit and fired the *Voyager*'s forward beams at it. She wasn't shooting to kill; just enough to let them know that her ship was bigger, and had teeth.

The Primacy ship boosted to avoid being a stationary target, and then *Voyager*'s scan suite screamed a warning about incoming projectiles.

<Launching chaff!> Katrina announced. *<Firing EM countermeasures.>*

Troy didn't respond, but the attitude thrusters fired and the *Voyager* changed trajectory, slamming Katrina sideways in her seat.

She glanced over to see that the case holding the antimatter was still secure before firing the beams at two missiles that had made it through the chaff and EM fields.

One missile detonated, but the other was still approaching.

Troy shifted trajectory again, putting the missile right behind them. The engine wash hit the incoming weapon, and it detonated a kilometer behind the *Voyager*.

<Nice try, assholes,> Troy said as he altered the ship's trajectory once more and spooled out the AP drive's nozzle.

<*I guess there's no reason not to burn Perseus,*> Katrina said. <*No one lives there.*>

<*My thinking as well,*> Troy said in agreement as he powered up the annihilator and the ship's velocity increased.

<*Just don't go over thirty gees,*> Katrina said as her armor filled her mouth with gel to keep her teeth from shattering. Elsewhere, it threaded nanostrands into her body, strengthening her bones against both the force and her body's two-ton weight.

<*Ship's only rated for twenty-five,*> Troy replied as he pushed it past twenty-six.

Katrina didn't even have the ability to give a rueful laugh as she pulled up the view of the patrol ship behind them. It had given up on pursuit and was circling around Perseus, back to the Evac Site—likely to rescue the soldiers on the surface.

<*We're not being followed,*> Katrina said, feeling the bullet in her side begin to travel back through her body. If her mouth hadn't been full of gel, she would have screamed.

<*I know, but I want to get our* v *up before we go dark.*>

<*Dark?*> she asked as tears filled her eyes. <*How dark?*>

<*This ship was meant as an ark to get to another habitable system, if needs be—which needs might be, indeed. Looks like Tanis wanted to be sure it could slip in unnoticed wherever it ended up.*>

<*Great. How good?*>

<*Stealth's as good as the* Andromeda*'s,*> Troy replied a happy tone to his normally dour voice.

Katrina brought up a view of the Kap System. If they could boost this hard, then alter their vector and go dark, it would be possible to slip past the sensors at the system's heliopause, and make it out into interstellar space undetected.

Which would be very useful, because if the patrol ship at Perseus wasn't pursuing them, it meant that the Primacy

Space Force had cruisers at the edge of the system moving to intercept the *Voyager*.

<*Stand by for another vector shift,*> Troy announced, and Katrina was pushed to the other side of her seat, and blinding pain coursed through her body as she felt at least two ribs snap.

<*Troy, no more, I can't…*>

<*Killing thrust, we're adrift.*>

Katrina attempted to breathe a sigh of relief, but pain stabbed through her in a dozen locations. She clenched her jaw and looked up the time to reach the heliopause: three days.

She reached up and unsealed her helmet, hooking it on her armor's chest. Spitting out the hardened gel in her mouth made her gag, but she managed, and began to undo her harness.

"I'm going to get this antimatter into storage, and then spend some time in the autodoc."

<*Yeah, you look like crap.*>

"Thanks."

Katrina turned and saw that the antimatter case was no longer in the seat next to her. She craned her head anxiously while fumbling with her harness.

"Fuuuuuuck," she breathed as she caught sight of it wedged between a console and the cockpit's bulkhead, dented, but otherwise undamaged.

<*I didn't mention it—figured you didn't need that stress,*> Troy said with a soft laugh. <*But if I could have crapped myself, I would have when it tore free.*>

Katrina let out a nervous chuckle. "I can imagine."

She pulled herself out of the seat and drifted toward the case in the zero-*g* environment. She gave a gentle tug and it didn't budge.

"Here goes nothing," Katrina said as she placed her feet on the deck and engaged the armor's maglocks. "This is gonna hurt…. One, two, three—"

There was a deafening screech, and the case came free. Katrina was glad she was wearing the armor, or she and the case would have gone flying across the cockpit.

Her eyes watered from the pain in her chest, and Katrina kept her breathing shallow as she examined the case. It was bent along one side, and she decided not to open it until she got to the engineering compartment. Chances were that it wouldn't close properly again, and the last thing she needed were five cylinders of antimatter floating around.

Utilizing her armor's maglocks, she walked down the ladder, moving perpendicular to each deck until she reached the bottom of the ship. There, she located the antimatter storage compartment and gently prised the case open.

There they were: five small containers, each with the potential to destroy a fleet of ships or to sterilize a planet. It was also the thing that would give the *Voyager* the ability to reach their destination in just six months.

With exacting care, she pulled each cylinder free and transferred it into a waiting receptacle. Once they were all in place, and the storage system sealed up, she took a step back and sagged in her armor.

"What a day…"

EMPTY

STELLAR DATE: 03.07.4331 (Adjusted Gregorian)
LOCATION: *Voyager*
REGION: Interstellar Space, Rimward of Kapteyn's Star

"Still nothing," Katrina said with a sigh as the probe's latest sensor sweep came back.

After spending half a year in stasis—during which Troy had silently drifted past the cruisers patrolling the edge of The Kap's heliosphere—they had reached the point where the *Intrepid* had disappeared.

Neither of them had expected to find anything at that location. The scout ships that had searched there a decade earlier had not found any signs, either.

But now they were a light year further along the *Intrepid*'s course, and there was still not a single sign of damage, or even stray ions floating in space. Although, finding ions from the engines twenty-eight years later was a pipe-dream at best.

<*We can press on further,*> Troy offered, <*or we can start up a grid.*>

"If they're under thrust, we'd see them, and if they're dead in space, we could search a thousand years and never find them," Katrina replied.

<*It just doesn't make any sense,*> Troy said, sounding more frustrated than Katrina had ever heard him. <*Even if something catastrophic had happened, they could have blown pods; hell, they could have blown the cylinders off to save the colonists. There should be ships, there should be…*>

Troy's voice faded, and Katrina knew how he felt.

"Hey, there's that weird graviton reading again; the probe picked up a bunch of them, too. What could they be from?"

Troy grunted over the Link. <*Beats me; galaxies colliding on the far side of the universe?*>

"The scout ships had found some gravitational disturbances, but they were stronger then. They too had assumed that the origin was a wave of gravitons from some distant event, but the wave never passed through the Kap System itself," Katrina said as she pulled up the relevant records.

<I recall, it was rather puzzling,> Troy said. *<I was always in the dark matter camp.>*

Katrina compared the readings that their probe had picked up to what the scout ships had found.

"What, that passing dark matter of some sort had created the waves?" she asked, only half paying attention to the conversation as she examined the readings.

<Yeah, but that dark matter was not in our space-time, but rather in some sub-layer of space; it occupies different dimensions, but gravity overlaps into our space-time.>

"Yeah, but there's no proof of that," Katrina said.

<Well, there's some. Just look at that research beaming out of Procyon these days.>

Katrina shrugged; there was that. The work on creating graviton emitters in Procyon—that the researchers there were freely beaming out to all of humanity—was groundbreaking. Many researchers were starting to use gravity to search for other physical dimensions in space-time, ones that were similar to the three that humans occupied.

"What are you suggesting, Troy?"

<Well, we know that Kapteyn's Star is extragalactic in origin, and spends most of its time far above or below the Milky Way's disk.>

"Right, we teach that to kids in school. Someday, their dozen-times great grandchildren will look up in the night sky and see the galaxy hanging above them—which will be breathtaking, I imagine."

<Right, The Kap is a halo star. It also has two major planets, Albion and Victoria, that it picked up along the way. But why? It doesn't have enough mass to pluck worlds out of the dark. Not at the speed it's moving through space.>

"Ohhh, I've heard this, it's the Streamer Theory," Katrina said with a nod.

<Yes!> Troy replied. *<The more I look at the original scout ship's data, and our probe's, the more I wonder if that theory is true.>*

"That theory says that The Kap pulls a supermassive string of dark matter along behind it that it picks up during its extragalactic transit through the galaxy's halo," Katrina said with a frown. "But if that's the case, and the *Intrepid* encountered it, then where is it? And why didn't they see it?"

<Well, I know the answer to the first question,> Troy said.

"You know where this dark matter streamer is?"

<Yes, right where it always was.>

Katrina snorted. "Troy, stop being coy and spit it out. I don't have the patience to play a guessing game."

<Fine, sorry, I got carried away. Remember, The Kap moves fast. If you were to leave The Kap today and encounter the Streamer, it would not be in the same place as it was when the Intrepid *would have encountered it.>*

"We're searching in the wrong place!" Katrina shouted.

<Yes, that is what I'm saying. The Streamer, if it's real, is sixty AU spinward of here…at least.>

"Do you think the *Intrepid* is stuck in it?" Katrina asked.

<That, or they're still travelling inside it, but its gravity is bending their tight-beams back to The Kap, so that we aren't getting their messages.>

"Troy, if you had a body, I'd hug you!" Katrina exclaimed. "I had always feared we'd never find them…I was starting to give into that."

<Well, don't get too excited yet; this is still just a theory,> Troy cautioned.

"I'm going to go take a shower and go down for a nap," Katrina said as she rose from her seat in the cockpit.

<Sweet dreams,> Troy replied.

A 'nap' was the term that Katrina had adopted for going into stasis. At first she thought that she would stay awake the entire time they searched, but it had been years since they had left The Kap, and she found herself staying out of stasis for increasingly short periods.

She did, however, luxuriate for a solid half hour under the hot spray of water before flipping the shower to its dry mode. Once dry, she walked across the hall to the stasis chamber and pulled a stasis suit from the rack.

The suit wasn't strictly necessary—the *Voyager* had true stasis pods, not cryostasis like the *Hyperion* had for the trip from Sirius. The suit, however, allowed the stasis pod to snap her in and out of stasis periodically, and get an instant reading on her health.

She pulled on the suit and then sat on the edge of the pod, staring at the wall of the stasis chamber.

"Do you regret this?" she asked softly, knowing that Troy would be listening.

<Not for a moment. I've been dismayed, yes. Annoyed at our lack of results, certainly. But never have I regretted. Can you imagine staying at The Kap and just waiting…waiting another forty years to hear if they made it?>

Katrina shook her head. "I don't know if I would have made it this long."

<You and me both, and I plan to live forever,> Troy replied.

"Wake me if you need me," Katrina said as she settled into the pod. As she got comfortable, she wondered briefly about Laura and how she was faring back at The Kap. Katrina hoped that the young woman had moved on with her life.

Living in the past was no way to live.

Katrina grew still; the pod sensed her readiness and slid the lid shut. She saw the readout give a five second countdown and read the numbers, *5…4…3…2…1….*

THE SEARCH

STELLAR DATE: 08.17.4352 (Adjusted Gregorian)
LOCATION: Primacy Capitol Buildings, Constance
REGION: Victoria, Kapteyn Primacy, Kapteyn's Star System

***Twenty-two years since Katrina departed in the* Voyager...**

Chancellor Laura rose from her chair and walked to the windows of her office. Below her, lay the planet Victoria, and beyond that, The Kapteyn Primacy. It was strong, it was secure; her people were unified and building a civilization that would be the envy of any star system—save Sol, perhaps.

And yet she felt so very empty.

The latest reports had come in. There was no sign of Kat's ship. Just like the *Intrepid* before it, the *Voyager* was gone. Not long after, a message had arrived from the FGT. The terraformers declared the *Intrepid* to be lost, disappeared without a trace.

Laura knew that whatever fate had befallen the *Intrepid* must have also taken Katrina. If the greatest colony ship ever built was obliterated by whatever lay in the darkness between Kapteyn's Star and New Eden, then there was no reason to hope that the *Voyager* would have fared any better.

A tightness grew in Laura's throat as she remembered the years she had spent as Katrina's assistant; how the woman had given her guidance and support without hesitation, even when she had been feeling a deep sadness herself.

Laura's eyes stung as hot tears spilled down her cheeks, and a sob tore free from her throat. She laid the side of her head against the window and gasped for breath as long moans of despair tore free from her throat.

She had never told Kat how she really felt.

And now that opportunity would never come.

Laura let herself cry until there was nothing left. She had to get it out now, before the press called her for a quote, and before she had to write a speech for Katrina's state funeral.

But for now, for however long she had, Laura would stare out at the world that Katrina had been so instrumental in building, and know that so long as she was here, so long as she was able, she would carry on Katrina's legacy and guide the worlds that drifted in the warm, ruddy glow of Kapteyn's Star.

CRASH

STELLAR DATE: UNKNOWN
LOCATION: *Voyager*
REGION: UNKNOWN

The cover to Katrina's pod slid open, and she was immediately assaulted by the sound of a klaxon blaring and the sight of emergency lights flashing. All around her, the ship shuddered like a groundcar riding down a washboard gravel road.

"Troy! What's happening!"

<*I think I found the Streamer!*> Troy replied, his voice anxious, but not panicked.

"I'm on my way up," Katrina said. "Can you kill the alarms, though? It's deafening."

<*Sorry, I always forget about things like that,*> Troy replied and a moment later, the blaring sound and flashing lights stopped.

Now that Katrina could think straight, she climbed out of the pod and pulled herself through the zero-*g* environment to the ladder shaft.

Traversing the ladder shaft was no simple task as the ship continued to shake around her. Several times she lost her grip and slammed into the bulkhead. Then, as she entered the cockpit, the shaking ceased, and she looked out the forward view to see only darkness.

"Uh, Troy, where'd space go?" she asked while settling into her seat and fastening the harness.

<*Good question,*> Troy replied. <*For a moment there was a tiny point of light ahead, and then it was gone.*>

"Nooo…" Katrina whispered. "Troy, that's not possible. Seriously, stop messing with me."

<*I wish I were,*> Troy said, his tone genuinely bewildered.

"But…that would imply we're going faster than the speed of light—which isn't possible," Katrina said absently as she reviewed the scan data—which showed nothing at all outside the ship.

<*It's not possible in space that is governed by general or special relativity; but there's no light here, that I can see, so why would it be a speed limit?*>

Katrina rubbed her eyes, feeling like she needed to go take another shower to wake up—even though she had taken one right before her nap. "So where are we, then?"

<*The calculations I've run show that—if it were in the right configuration—a string of massive dark matter could create a lens that would pull us out of regular space-time, and put us into some sub-layer of space…or over-layer.*>

"Troy," Katrina began cautiously. "'Gravity lens' sounds suspiciously like 'wormhole'."

<*I wondered if you'd notice that,*> Troy replied. <*I suspect it will have not dissimilar properties.*>

"So how do we get out of it?" Katrina asked.

<*Or do we even try?*> Troy responded.

Katrina let out nervous laugh. "What do you mean?"

<*Think about it, Katrina. If the* Intrepid *fell into this Streamer, then we should follow it and see where it goes. That's where they'll be.*>

"Or they tried to get out," Katrina said. "Do you think they would just stay in this thing to see where it goes?"

<*Good point,*> Troy said. <*I suppose they would try to get out. Perhaps to move the ship laterally.*>

"Should we try the probe?" Katrina asked.

<*Yes, why not? We have three of them; we can push this one out and see if it makes the transition smoothly—if there is anywhere to transition to.*>

"You're so full of encouraging statements," Katrina said.

<Sorry, but this **is** *fascinating, you know. We could be some of the first people to travel faster than light!>*

Katrina nodded slowly. It was amazing, but all she could think of was them flying past the *Intrepid,* and coming out of this wormhole somewhere ridiculous—like the Andromeda galaxy.

"Yeah, we'd be some of the first…if you failed to count the two and a half million people on the *Intrepid*."

<Well, one of the first ships, then. OK, launching the probe in ten seconds.>

Katrina pulled the probe's sensor feed up, in addition to the *Voyager*'s exterior view, and watched as the small, oval probe drifted away from the ship's port side.

It experienced only minor gravitational fluctuations as it travelled; then, when it was eleven kilometers away, it disappeared.

"No debris," Katrina said as she reviewed the data.

<There one second, and gone the next. I was worried about shearing forces at the edge, but there don't appear to be any.>

"On this side," Katrina whispered.

Neither of them spoke for a minute. Then Troy finally replied. *<So, are we going to do this?>*

Katrina nodded slowly. "Yes…yes, let's. If they're nowhere to be found, we can always go back into the Streamer."

<Probably.>

She didn't reply; she knew what he meant. Even if they made it out, there was no way to know if the Streamer could be entered at any point, or if they would have to travel back to The Kap to slip inside once more.

<Fusion drive isn't doing anything in here; trying the AP…maybe the gamma rays can shift us over.>

The ship's status board showed the AP drive's nozzle spooling out, and the antimatter annihilation began. Usually an AP burn was accompanied by a feeling of thrust, but this time there was barely anything.

Troy twisted the nozzle slowly, and the ship began to move toward the edge of the darkness. Or what they had to assume was the edge.

Once the *Voyager* gained momentum, Troy retracted the nozzle, and the ship drifted toward where the probe had exited.

Well, probably not the exact same place.

Even though there was no reference frame in this place, they had to be moving somewhere….

After only moving seven kilometers, a shudder traveled through the ship and suddenly, stars snapped into place around them.

Not only distant points of light, either; one was very close, only 70 AU, by the scan suite's quick estimate.

"Holy shit…" Katrina breathed. "We made it."

<*Yeah, but where?*>

Katrina watched the nav system attempt to match their position with any known charts, and fail.

<*Oh…I think I know what's wrong,*> Troy said in a strange voice, and Katrina watched him bring up the stars within a thousand light years from Sol on a chart, and then remove Betelgeuse.

The action caused a small shift in the positions of all the stars, and suddenly the stellar cartography system chimed as it identified their location.

They were at the edge of 58 Eridani, almost twenty-four light years from New Eden.

"Wha…I…" Katrina stammered.

<*I feel the same way,*> Troy said. <*By our clocks, we were in the Streamer for only half an hour; but we've travelled thirty five light years.*>

"You removed Betelgeuse…to make the stars match up," Katrina said, unable to process what that meant.

<*That's because it went nova…about a thousand years ago,*> Troy replied, and Katrina wondered if it was fear that she heard in his mental tone.

The stellar cartography system finished its assessment of stellar drift, matching it against nearby galaxies. The date that appeared on the nav system nearly made Katrina's heart stop.

- Current Date, Gregorian: 8511 -

BOLLAM'S WORLD

STELLAR DATE: 11.09.8511 (Adjusted Gregorian)
LOCATION: ***Voyager***
REGION: Edge of the Bollam's World System (58 Eridani)

Once the shock wore off, Katrina brought up the comm systems and initiated a passive scan of the star system they were on the edge of.

"I have radio signals coming off the system," Katrina said. "A *lot* of radio signals. I guess people have colonized this far out."

She could barely believe the words she was saying. Of course humans would have made it forty light years from Earth in the intervening four thousand years.

<*I hear it as well,*> Troy said. <*I'm listening for any mention of the* Intrepid, *or any signals from it…*>

Katrina knew what Troy left unsaid.

If they had jumped this far through space and time, an expectation that the *Intrepid* had exited anywhere close to the same location in both time and place was unrealistic.

If they had exited the Streamer in the same millennia, it would be a miracle.

"What do we do, Troy?" Katrina asked. "Do we go insystem?"

<*I don't know,*> Troy said after a few moments of silence. <*Maybe not. We don't know anything about who these people are. I think we should go dark and just listen for a bit.*>

"Seems prudent," Katrina said as she spotted a strange pattern in a familiar range of the EM spectrum. She isolated it and pulled the signal into the comm systems.

<*That's some serious encryption on that message,*> Troy said.

"Yeah," Katrina whispered in a shaky voice.

<*What is it?*> Troy asked.

"That's…that's Sirian encryption."

<*Are you kidding? Are you sure?*>

Neither of them knew exactly what it meant—Sirians being in 58 Eridani, four thousand years in the future—but it couldn't be good.

Katrina tried her old keys from her time as a spy for the Lumins and found that they opened the outer layer of the message, revealing the header and meta data.

"Well, now we know the name of this place," Katrina said. "Bollam's World."

Troy's tone was derisive. <*Who names a system 'world'?*>

"I'm seeing something really weird on scan," Katrina said.

<*Define 'weird'.*> Troy replied.

"Well, two ships just disappeared not far from here…"

A view of the system appeared on the cockpit's main holodisplay, and a marker highlighted a point half an AU from the *Voyager*.

<*Was it here?*> Troy asked.

"Yeah…ohhhhhh."

Katrina felt her mouth go dry as she read the label on the marker: 'Jump Point 4A – New Eden'.

Neither of them spoke, and then another ship disappeared from Scan before two others appeared from nowhere. All the ships were appearing and disappearing at various locations around the periphery of the system, none closer than 50 AU to the Bollam's World's star.

<*I can only surmise one thing,*> Troy said eventually.

Katrina drew in a deep breath and fell back into her seat. "Me too. They have FTL. Troy…I…I don't even know how to process this. I'm going to make some coffee."

<*I wish you could make some for me too,*> Troy replied. <*I'll keep listening in on what I can…maybe there will be some mention of the* Intrepid.>

Katrina pulled off her harness and pushed herself back down the ladder shaft to Deck #3 where the galley was located. Once she reached it, she paused and surveyed the room.

It was meant to seat over fifty people—the *Voyager* being intended to carry all three hundred of the Gamma Site's personnel.

The large, empty space had always felt lonely while they were searching for the *Intrepid,* but now…now it felt worse. The *Intrepid* could have arrived at Bollam's World hundreds of years ago. Or it could have shot past, and be further out, maybe as far as the Orion Nebula.

She had felt so certain that they would find the *Intrepid,* that in just a few years, she'd be sitting at Tanis's kitchen table in her cabin by Ol' Sam's lake.

Now it felt like she had an entire galaxy to search.

Sorrow and despair suffused Katrina, and the emotions she had been holding in check for so long threatened to drown her. She placed a hand against the bulkhead, gripping a handhold as tears flowed from her eyes, forming small salty droplets all around her.

She let herself wallow in the sadness for just a minute before choking back the tears and wiping her face. There would be time enough for regret later. For now, she would allow herself a cup of coffee, and a snack of some sort, and then she needed to rejoin Troy in studying the system's feeds.

Katrina reached one of the storage units and pulled out a packet of coffee. In zero-*g* she couldn't brew it properly, so the instant suck-pack would have to do.

While the packet was heating up in the prep unit, she pulled some chips out of a cupboard and prised open the container. It was close to the last of the real food. Soon enough she'd be on paste.

Unless we go into this system…

There weren't a lot of options. They needed more intel, and floating around out here wasn't going to get it for them. What's more, if these people really did have FTL, then determining if the *Voyager* could be upgraded to support it was high on the list of priorities.

The incongruity of being in a ship that had just—maybe—travelled faster than light, now needing an upgrade to travel faster than light was not lost on Katrina.

She pulled the coffee packet out of the prep unit and uncapped the straw, taking a long pull of the bitter, not particularly pleasant brew.

<We've been pinged.> Troy said. *<It's an STC NSAI wondering why we're not on a standard approach vector.>*

"I thought you went dark?" Katrina asked aloud.

<That takes a bit of work; I was running through checks when it reached out. It's only five light minutes away.>

"And it's just 'wondering'?" Katrina asked aloud.

<Well, it's actually ordering us to declare our destination so it can assign us an approach vector.>

"I'm on my way back up," Katrina replied.

While she drifted up the ladder shaft, she reviewed the nearby habs and stations.

The system sported two habitable worlds, and there was a third, that may be in the early stages of terraforming, in orbit of the sixth planet, a large jovian listed as Kithari on the scan data.

That world was too deep in the system to visit, but the twelfth planet, a rock and ice plutino, had a number of stations near it. One was named 'Tsarina Commerce District #3'.

Not too creative, but it looks well trafficked. Perhaps we can blend in there.

When she reached the cockpit, Troy already had the facility up on the holo.

<*Saw you looking at this place's specs,*> he said as she drifted toward her seat.

"Yeah, it seemed like a good candidate," Katrina replied. "I didn't really look at a lot of details."

<*It's as good as any of the others,*> Troy replied. <*I'll tell the NSAI that we're heading in, and then proceed about as slow as possible once we get a lane. Take as much time as we can to soak up whatever we can about this place.*>

"Sounds solid," Katrina said in agreement.

As Troy communicated with the STC NSAI—who he referred to as 'surly' more than once—Katrina discovered that the beacons on the edge of the system could be queried for various databases with history, culture, and trade information.

The closest beacon was fifteen light minutes away, and a half hour later, Katrina was browsing the Bollam's World Tourism Department's welcome packet.

What she found flabbergasted her.

The Bollam's World System *had* been colonized by Sirians, by a ship named the GSS *Yewing*. The name was familiar, and she dredged up memories of the *Yewing* from her school days.

The *Yewing* had left Sirius in 3814, supposedly travelling to Alula Australis where it had been granted a world to settle in the Future Generation Terraformer controlled system.

Katrina had always wondered why the FGT had opened up a world to the Sirians, of all people. She'd long harbored a suspicion that the Generation Ship Service had never made the world available to the *Yewing*—and that its destination was just another lie the Lumin government had perpetrated on the Sirian people.

In the end, it hadn't mattered, the GSS *Yewing* had never made it to Alula Australis; it had been declared lost in 4012. Yet somehow, the *Yewing* had hit Kapteyn's streamer and ended up here.

Katrina pulled up the stellar cartography suite. She knew that there was no way that Kapteyn's Streamer passed anywhere near the *Yewing*'s route to Alula Australis—which meant the ship had always been headed elsewhere.

It wouldn't have surprised her to find that the *Yewing* had always been destined for New Eden with a plan to snatch the system from whomever it was legally assigned to.

However, it seemed that the *Yewing* had hit the Streamer as well, and arrived at Bollam's World in 5123. At that time, the system had a few settlements and no terraformed worlds. The records made brief note of clearing out existing settlements before beginning terraforming work.

Katrina suspected she knew what the nature of that 'clearing out' had been. She bet that the *Yewing*'s colonists got to enact their plans of forcibly stealing a system after all.

And now, four thousand years later, they were still here.

Which meant that they knew about the Streamer, and possibly where ships would likely exit it. Though maybe exit points were effectively random, and no one would be looking—especially with ships appearing and disappearing via FTL all the time.

<*Got our lane,*> Troy said as Katrina was examining the cultural differences between the people of Bollam's World and the Sirians. Unfortunately, there was far too much of Luminescent Society's attitudes and behaviors present in Bollam's World. The underclass was more integrated, but otherwise it was almost a mirror of Sirius.

"We've just arrived, and already I'm looking forward to getting out of here," Katrina replied.

<*That may take a bit, but not as long as I'd feared. It appears as though faster-than-light travel is facilitated through graviton emitters, which I guess those folks in Procyon finally figured out. Ships transition into this place called the dark layer, where they move really fast,*> Troy said.

"Oh, yeah? How fast?"

<*It varies, but the average seems to be five hundred times faster than the speed of light.*>

"Sweet starlight, that's fast," Katrina whispered. "I guess people can go pretty much anywhere now…it wouldn't even be three weeks to get back to The Kap. I wonder—"

<*Don't,*> Troy said ominously.

"Don't what?" Katrina asked, suspecting what Troy was going to say, but hopeful it was something else.

<*Don't look up The Kap—or anything to do with it. Save it for another time.*>

Curiosity burned in Katrina's mind, but she could tell by Troy's statement that he was serious, and that wondering was probably better than knowing—for now.

<*The thing we need to sort out is how we can pay for an FTL upgrade. This ship isn't suited for cargo, otherwise I'd advocate that we do some in-system hauls for a bit and—oh, damn…*>

"What is it?" Katrina asked.

<*I had been assuming that their level of tech was above ours, what with FTL. But it's not; I think they're barely thirtieth millennia by comparison.*>

Katrina let that sink in for a minute before replying. "What are they missing?"

<*Their nanotech is garbage. They don't have stasis capabilities; their life spans are a lot shorter. I wonder if it's just this system that is so backward, or if it's like this everywhere.*>

"Are these graviton emitters all that's more advanced?" Katrina asked.

<*Well, graviton emitters make for some amazing technology. For starters, they have artificial gravity on their ships, inertial dampeners—which I bet your ribs would have liked to have had when we left Perseus.*>

"You can say that again," Katrina interjected.

<*They also don't need to rotate stations; though they often still do, since it's cheaper. Oh, and they can make antimatter with ease,*> Troy concluded.

"I think we'll need to hide that we're from the past," Katrina said. "That we have better tech than they do in so many ways puts us at risk."

<*Crap.*> Troy muttered. <*They have gravity-based engines and shields too. At our tonnage, when we get close to the station, we have to come in on grav drives only.*>

Katrina sighed. "Which we don't have."

<*I can fake a failure of some sort,*> Troy said.

"I don't know," Katrina said. "Feels too risky. I think that perhaps I should take the pinnace into the station and have you move further out…preferably stealthed."

<*That may be prudent,*> Troy said after a moment's silence. <*If they don't have stasis tech, then they probably don't have advanced stealth tech. I can probably sneak right under their noses.*>

"Sounds like a plan."

<*Now I just have to explain to that unpleasant NSAI that we've changed our minds, and to transfer our lane to the pinnace. I bet it'll be a joy.*>

*****

Katrina settled into the cockpit of the *Victory*'s small pinnace, and pulled herself down into one of the two seats before triggering the cockpit's canopy to close over her.

Though the pinnace was small, it was well equipped. Behind the cockpit was a cabin with bunks for two, a small weapons locker, and even a san with a water shower. It also had beams that were more than just defensive, though she didn't know what they would do against gravity shields.

In theory, such a shield could simply bend light away. She wondered if weapons in the eighty sixth century had upgraded as well to pack more punch.

The final feature of the pinnace was an ability to manage planetary landings, although she hoped not to need that ability on this trip.

<You take care,> Troy said. *<I really don't like the idea of you being alone out there.>*

"You worry too much, Troy," Katrina replied. "You're turning into a crotchety old grandmother."

<You recall that six hours ago we were in the forty fourth century, right? I feel like this is like what you organics would call a 'nightmare'. So I hope you'll forgive me for worrying.>

Katrina sighed as she fastened her harness. Troy was right; everything was turned on its head. Separating felt crazy, but no other plan had any higher chance of success.

"There's some serendipity," Katrina said. "The way they're holding onto Sirian customs here, I'll be able to blend right in. Don't forget, I spent thirty years as a spy back in Sirius. Given the nanotech these people have, I should be able to do whatever I please down there."

<Don't get cocky, Katrina. You and I, we're alone in this universe now. We're the only ones who have the other's back.>

"If all goes well, I'll be back in seven days. If it takes longer, I'll get a message to you."

<You'd better,> Troy said. *<Don't make me have to fly in there and save you.>*

Katrina smiled. Troy was a good friend, and he meant what he said. It felt good to know he had her back.

TSARINA COMMERCE DISTRICT #3

STELLAR DATE: 11.13.8511 (Adjusted Gregorian)
LOCATION: Bay 1342, Tsarina Commerce District #3 (station)
REGION: Tsarina, Bollam's World System (58 Eridani)

Katrina eased the pinnace into the bay designated by Tsarina station's STC. The ship drifted through the grav shield that stretched across the bay's entrance, and she felt a slight jolt as the station's graviton-powered docking system took over.

She powered down the vessel's chem thrusters and watched a cradle rise out of the deck ahead, ready to accept the ship.

Through the pinnace's windows, she could see that the bay was mostly occupied by smaller craft; some shuttles and small freighters also rested on cradles nearby.

Amidst the ships stood stacks of cargo. Streams of passengers and service teams threaded their way between the stacks and the loaders who were ferrying crates to and from the various ships.

It was just the sort of organized chaos one would expect from such a place.

Something that *was* missing was the familiar gravity assisted cargo sorting systems. Normally, outbound cargo was dropped down to receiving ships from warehouses and the ships making deliveries, which would be positioned high up in the bay. Here it was just one flat bay, with cargo being moved on floating pads.

Another change graviton emitters had wrought.

Katrina barely noticed as her pinnace settled into the cradle, but she assumed the docking was complete, as a ramp rose from the deck and extended to the cockpit.

When it stopped, Katrina punched in the command for the cockpit to open. As the vessel equalized atmospheric pressure with the bay, she stood and stretched.

It was time to put on a show.

The woman who stepped out of the pinnace was not the same as the one who had entered it. This one was an aristocrat who was used to getting her way, and unwilling to suffer fools.

Katrina knew that the best way to maintain a cover was to become that cover. This cover had a name: Verisa.

Verisa was dressed for the part. Before leaving the *Voyager*, Katrina had used a fab unit to alter a stasis suit and create a skinsheath, which was the current style within the Bollam's World System.

The mode of dress was not entirely dissimilar to what she had worn back in Sirius—when she wasn't undercover on Noctus stations.

The stasis suit was a light blue, and fit snugly. Katrina had even managed to enhance it to emit a soft blue glow; though it wasn't capable of putting on the sort of light show that had been common back on Sirius—and may be required here to pass oneself off as a member of the upper class.

As she stood at the top of the ramp and surveyed those nearby, Katrina saw that few of the people present had clothing that glowed. She hoped that what she had managed with the stasis suit would suffice.

Her review of the bay complete, Katrina strode down the ramp toward a woman waiting at its foot.

"Weird hull configuration on your skiff," the woman said.

The woman wore the uniform of a Tsarina Station employee. A tight, green, one-piece suit with brown boots that came to her knees, a wide brown belt, and a broad yellow stripe down her right side and arm. The suit had a soft glow to it, and in the center of her chest was the Tsarina logo: four yellow concentric circles, with a red, upside down, equilateral triangle overtop. A pair of brown gloves hung from a hook on the woman's belt, along with a variety of tools and two datapads.

Handheld datapads; now that's archaic, Katrina mused.

However, the woman's outfit and equipment were not the most interesting features. Though the woman's face appeared normal—albeit rather pale—her head was topped with a ridged, steel cone. She looked as though someone had put the pointy end of a very large egg on her head.

From what Katrina could see, it wasn't a helmet or a hat; it *was* the woman's head. Her IR overlay showed that it was a few degrees warmer than the woman's skin, and had a large glowing red triangle on the front that matched the one on her uniform.

Modded that much to work the docks? Katrina wondered. *And with a mod that appears to be the property of Tsarina, as well.*

A glint of silver around the woman's neck caught Katrina's notice, and she realized that the woman was wearing a steel collar.

Her research while inbound had shown that many of the people in Bollam's World were indentured servants—some even slaves. *Perhaps this woman is amongst their ranks, and the collar is the sign of that status.*

All these thoughts raced through her mind in the time it had taken the woman to make her comment about Katrina's ship.

Katrina looked down her nose at the woman and gave a disdainful sniff. "Its configuration isn't that strange. Provided one gets out of this backwater from time to time."

The woman glanced up at Katrina and shrugged. "Yeah, well, that's not an option for me." She looked back down at her datapad. "Need anything? Fuel, refit? Antimatter to declare?"

Katrina shook her head. "No. I just need storage for a few days."

"Storage, got it. I have your token on record here. It's seven-hundred credits a day if you want to keep it on the cradle, or two hundred if we rack it."

Katrina had already reviewed the options. As much as she wanted to keep the pinnace ready to go, the station's bank had only granted her a forty-thousand credit on the bond for her pinnace. She couldn't have storage fees eating so much of her finite funds.

"Rack it," Katrina replied.

"You got it, the woman said. "I'll just need you to pass me the auxiliary codes for the pinnace so we can make sure engines and the like stay offline."

Katrina nodded and connected to the dock's net, seeking out the woman before her, and passing the necessary data.

"There you are," Katrina said. "Do you require anything else?"

"Nope. Dock security's already scanned you, so you're good to go."

"Very well," Katrina replied.

As she walked across the dock toward the broad passageway on the far side, she noticed that about half of the Tsarina employees seemed to have visible modifications, and most of those with the larger, less agreeable mods also wore collars.

Katrina connected to the broader station net and pulled up the locations of companies listing repair and upgrade services for a ship like the *Voyager*. She was hoping to find one with its own shipyard, or a mobile service vessel. Nothing good would come from bringing the *Voyager* insystem to one of the stations here—even if they could get around the grav drive issues.

Four results matched her query, and Katrina selected one that had a good mix of reviews. The company's sales office wasn't too far, and Katrina overlaid the route on her HUD as she walked out of the bay.

The corridor out of the docking bay had a designated lane for foot traffic, and Katrina walked slowly on the right side, studiously observing the other passersby in addition to the haulers floating through the center of the passage on their anti-gravity pads.

She couldn't help but marvel at the incongruity of such amazing technology as artificial gravity, while also seeing people with visible, and highly inefficient, mods built into their bodies.

More than a few of the people she passed even possessed un-skinned artificial limbs, ill-fitting poly-skin, and even metallic, non-organic-looking eyes.

It was like the worst sort of slum back in Sirius; one where the people would take whatever work they could to keep from being sent to the Noctus mining platforms.

After one hundred meters, the passageway emptied out into a wide boulevard that swept around the station—the curve visible far in the distance on both sides. Here she saw a higher percentage of people with fewer unappealing mods.

What she also noticed was that her dimly glowing outfit was both not tight enough, and didn't glow nearly bright enough for her to be taken as upper class on Tsarina station. It also lacked the requisite light shows cascading across her body.

It really is just like Luminescent Society. How is my past waiting for me this far in the future?

Katrina knew that in a society this stratified, her clothing meant as much as her money—especially when it came to negotiating for the work on the *Voyager*. Her current outfit painted her as middle class at best. Nowhere near where she needed to be.

A quick check of the station's layout showed her where the more expensive shops lay, and a ten-minute walk followed by a five-minute maglev ride took her to a wide boulevard lined with high-end shops.

It had always amused Katrina that while most people professed to believe that living in space was better than living on planets, they always strove to make their most pleasant spaces look like they were planet-side.

This place, proclaimed as Lourmis Boulevard by a tasteful sign nestled amongst some low bushes, was no different. Above the wide street, there was no ceiling: just a blue expanse with white clouds and a bright yellow sun. It was almost good enough to fool Katrina; but her newly augmented eyes—courtesy of the rejuv—could pick up on irregularities, and the excessive symmetry told her it was a holoprojection—which was obvious, anyway, since they were inside a station 47 AU from the star.

Below the blue sky, the center of the boulevard was lined with tall oaks, and each of the quaint little shops was nestled amongst more trees—all of which was backed by a holographic forest that seemed to stretch on to the horizon.

The people here, clearly the upper echelon of the station, possessed no visible mods whatsoever. Katrina wondered if they were vanilla, or simply had access to better, more discrete technology than the working class down at the docks.

She let out a long sigh and drew herself up. It was time to fully embrace the thing she hated most. The trappings of Luminescent Society.

An hour later, the woman who walked back to the docks no longer bore any resemblance to Katrina. She was now Verisa, through and through.

Her body was adorned in a gleaming black skinsheath with red accents that had a bight, yet somehow sinister glow to them as they traced patterns across her body. Periodically the red accents would widen, and appear to expose raging fires within.

The outfit covered her right up to her chin, with a cutout above her breasts that appeared to be a hole into some hellish dimension.

The effect made it look as though her body was actually made of flame, with a glistening black covering twisting and writhing in an attempt to cover the inferno beneath.

To further enhance the look, the salesperson had dusted a powder filled with tiny light projectors in her hair. Now her red locks sparkled and glowed, periodically appearing to burst into flame.

Her lips were also a deep red, with light dancing across them, and her green eyes glowed eerily, courtesy of a simple alteration Katrina made with her own nano.

All of that was difficult to see with the large black hood pulled over her head—something that Verisa loved, as it added mystery to her appearance. It shrouded her eyes, but showed her sparkling red lips all too clearly.

Even Katrina had to admit that the outfit was astounding. It had better be, for the fortune it had cost her. But the impressive effects were nothing compared to her new boots.

Jet-black and ending just above her knees, the boots possessed no heel, but held her feet pointed straight down. Had she actually been walking in them, Katrina was certain the footwear would be both excruciating and ungainly.

However, tiny—yet powerful—antigravity generators in the boots held the tips of her toes ten centimeters off the ground, while evenly supporting her legs within, as she took her lazily floating steps along the boulevard.

She had told herself that the expensive purchase was necessary in order to research the small graviton emitters in the boots, should negotiations for upgrades fall through.

It wasn't a complete lie; it would be interesting to see how the tech was miniaturized—but Katrina knew she probably would have bought the boots anyway. The opportunity to walk on air was simply too fascinating to pass up.

The incredible outfit and the ability to simply glide through the air made it easy to maintain the Verisa persona. She was a powerful and dangerous woman; she could afford to spend more on whimsical clothing than most people earned in a month.

When she reached the maglev platform, a train was pulling up, and she drifted aboard. She wanted to stand, but knew that a woman of her position would not do so. She settled into a seat, forcing herself not to idly bounce her feet on air in front of her, when a conversation a few seats away piqued her interest.

"...last of the ones from that ship are up for auction soon," a man in a gleaming purple and blue skinsheath said to another man who was wearing a Tsarina uniform—though his stripe was golden rather than yellow, and no collar encircled his neck.

"I heard about that," the second man said. "Just the dregs, I expect; though I'm amazed there were so many people aboard. Usually ships coming through the streamer are a lot smaller."

Katrina had searched the records multiple times for mention of the *Intrepid;* though once she saw the level of technology in the Bollam's World System, she was certain the colony ship had not exited the Streamer here.

However, the mention of a ship with a lot of people aboard piqued her interest—even though it was unlikely to be the *Intrepid*.

"Yeah, wasn't a good selection to start with," the man in the purple and blue said. "They were refugees from the wars in the Pleiades—that place is practically trashed right now. Not a lot of anything of value coming out of there."

The man in the Tsarina uniform nodded. "True, but I did get two new dockworkers from one of the lots. They're collared and earning their keep now."

"Good; probably the best thing that's happened to them their whole miserable lives."

The conversation sickened Katrina; the way the two men talked about other people as though they were of little more value than furniture.

She felt for the refugees. It wasn't so long ago—in the grand scheme of things, at least—that she had been a refugee, along with everyone else aboard the *Hyperion.*

I'm not far off from that status, now.

The two men continued to talk about the tech pulled from the ship from the Pleiades, and what the hull would sell for, while the maglev travelled to the commercial section of the station.

When the train reached her stop, Katrina rose and exited, and the two men followed after. She could feel their eyes on her, a fact she confirmed with a few nanoprobes that she released to watch them.

One of the men was openly staring at her ass, his eyes never wavering for an instant as he talked to his friend. Katrina was wondering if she would have to fend off more than just their eyes, when they turned down a side-passage, their voices lost in the crowds on the platform.

While Katrina didn't care for their behavior, Verisa couldn't help a small smirk. Verisa moved as though she was in command of everyone around her, and they existed to serve at her pleasure. That those two men found her irresistible meant that Katrina was playing the part properly.

From the maglev station, it only took Katrina a few minutes to reach the sales office of the company she had selected before her excursion to Lourmis Boulevard.

A blue and purple holodisplay above the entrance proudly displayed the company's name to all passersby: 'KiStar Interstellar'.

KiStar specialized in onsite work, and had a fleet of service vessels, which was perfect—if she could secure their services. There was one thing that Katrina still didn't have a plan for: how she would pay them.

The *Voyager* possessed no small amount of technology that she could trade—from its superior fusion drives, to its advanced neural computer, stasis, and stealth systems. However, Katrina wasn't entirely certain that empowering anyone in the Bollam's World System with the *Voyager*'s advanced tech was the best course of action.

She wondered for a moment if her dislike for the people of Bollam's World was due to their heritage, or to how they operated with indentured servants and allowed slavery.

Probably a combination.

They were all really just one step above pirates, as far as Katrina was concerned...maybe not even that. Pirates, for the most part, owned up to what they were.

Even if she did want to trade technology, the difference between possessing a piece of tech, and having the ability to reproduce it, were not even close to the same things.

And that was a problem.

Neither she nor Troy had base design specifications for most of the technology onboard the *Voyager*. She had reviewed her options a dozen times, and the best she could come up with was to sell a number of the stasis pods in exchange for the upgrades.

Negotiating that, however, would be a delicate business.

She drew in a deep breath and strode through the open doors of KiStar Interstellar.

Once inside, she took special care not to marvel at the displays hovering above the deck on a-grav plinths. The incongruity of her amazement almost made her laugh aloud. She too was hovering above the deck.

Katrina 'walked' amidst the displays of engine components and scale models of ships until she spotted a woman who was sheathed in a glowing white outfit, complete with multiple instances of the blue and purple KiStar logo moving across her body. The logos grew, shrank, merged, and faded in and out. The effect was rather mesmerizing.

That's one way to liven up a uniform.

The KiStar employee was speaking with a woman who wore none of the local styles. Her body was covered in long, dark robes, and Katrina was surprised to see a sword hanging from a strap slung over her shoulders.

Perhaps Katrina, too, could have opted for some sort of outsystem attire—though she suspected it would be too hard to pull together enough information on cultures beyond Bollam's World to create a convincing disguise.

"May I help you?" a voice asked from behind her, and Katrina turned to see a man approaching. He was dressed in a uniform that matched the woman's, though his neck bore a silver collar.

"Yes," Katrina replied in Verisa's measured and dismissive voice. "Find someone who has the wherewithal to possess their own person. I do not speak with chattel."

As she spoke, the lines of fire on her skinsheath widened, the angry red glow around her intensifying.

The man took a step back and she waved her fingers at him as though she were brushing a piece of lint off her shoulder.

"Milady," the man said hurriedly, and she turned away, assuming he had withdrawn.

She waited, standing stock still save for a slow bounce as she hovered above the floor.

After a few minutes, the woman in the black robes left, and the other KiStar salesperson approached Katrina. Her eyes widened briefly as she took in Katrina's outfit.

"Ma'am, I'm Uriah. I understand that you wish to speak with me?"

Katrina turned and looked the woman over. Her blue hair matched the KiStar logos racing across her body, and her purple lips and eyes stood out from skin almost as pale as the white skinsheath she wore.

"I suppose you will be sufficient," Katrina said. "I wish to discuss a refit of my ship's grav systems. On my latest FTL jump, they suffered a failure and taxed my ship's reactor. The ship is old, but dear to me, and I wish to modernize all of its grav systems."

"How unfortunate!" Uriah exclaimed, her concern appearing very genuine. "Thankfully, you've come to the right place. KiStar specializes in grav systems, as you can see," the woman gestured to the many starship components hovering around the showroom. "May I ask what manufacturer and model your ship is?"

During the three-day approach to Tsarina, Katrina had researched the most obscure ship models she could, while still finding one that resembled the *Voyager* in some fashion. There were no good matches, but she had made the best selection she could.

"It's a Jasepsce Imperial 3110," Katrina replied, as though it were the most common ship in space.

"I'm sorry, a what?" Uriah asked, her delicate features registering consternation.

"The manufacturer is Jasepsce. They operate out of the Femier System. It's on the far side of the Genevian Alliance. I assume you've heard of it. I was told that your establishment had extensive expertise. That you were the best."

Uriah flushed, purple no less. Even when someone wasn't owned by their employer, it seemed that the companies took many liberties with the bodies of their staff.

After a moment, during which Uriah's eyes darted left to right several times, the woman nodded. "Ah yes, I have their information on file. Jasepsce. The Imperial model appears to be a light touring cruise ship, just under two-hundred meters long, and sixty-thousand tons, yes?"

Katrina nodded sharply. "The 3110 is a touch longer. But its tonnage is less. Only fifty-six."

"And you want a full refit of all grav systems?"

"I want you to tear out what's there and install your best model of graviton emitters. I want the works: drive, shields, dark layer transition field, dampeners. I'm not going to rely on three-hundred-year-old systems any longer," Katrina replied.

Uriah's eyes widened. "That is quite the undertaking. Is the ship in dock, Madam…?"

"You may call me Verisa. And no, my ship is thirty AU from here. While I quite admire your people's fashion, I am not prepared to bring a damaged ship into your system."

Uriah sighed, and Katrina wondered how many other people felt the same way about Bollam's World.

It was a relatively isolated system, with no other G-class stars within ten light years. However, it was situated at the intersection of several major empires—in a sort of no-man's land that no regional power wanted to enter, lest they disrupt the peace they shared with their neighbors.

It made Bollam's world useful, but also autonomous enough that they could do as they wished—or didn't wish.

Despite its veneer of civilization, Katrina's research had made her quite certain that the modus operandi within Bollam's heliosphere was 'to the victor go the spoils'.

"I understand," Uriah replied. "We do have service ships that can perform the work off station. However, doing so is more expensive, and will require a substantial deposit."

"How much is substantial?" Katrina asked, sounding disinterested.

"Thirty thousand credits. Due before our ship leaves dock. The rest of the payment is due once our Crew Chief assesses the work and provides you with the quote."

Katrina nearly choked. *Thirty thousand credits just to fly out and assess the work?* That would consume the vast majority of her available credit. She weighed the possibility of touring the other shops, but the reviews and comments on their listings had all led her to believe that KiStar was the least expensive of the lot.

Shopping around would also cause storage fees for the pinnace to consume much of her remaining funds.

"That is agreeable. Although, from what I can see of your repair fleet and the cost of fuel on this station, I believe that a deposit of twenty-five thousand is far more fitting."

Uriah's eyes darted to the side, and Katrina waited while the woman consulted with whomever oversaw such agreements.

"Very well. Will you be flying back out alone, or would you like to dock your pinnace within our repair ship for the flight?"

Uriah was marginally competent, then—or she had an NSAI researching Verisa while they spoke. Either way, Katrina was certain that the woman's offer was not a request. The pinnace would be leveraged as additional security on the service call, should Katrina not agree to KiStar's rate once they arrived at the *Voyager*.

"I will dock it within your vessel. I would like to discuss the work with your crew chief while we travel to my ship.

"Which is named?" Uriah asked.

"The *Voyager,*" Katrina replied.

"And how will you pay for the bulk of the repairs? I see that your accounts here are new."

Katrina did not want to tip her hand by exposing that she had advanced tech here on the station. Once out in the black, after she had worked out a way to influence the crew of the repair ship, then she would reveal her actual method of payment.

"I have Nietzschean Block-Chain Credits," she replied. "More than enough to cover the repairs."

"Nietzschean?" Uriah asked, and Katrina nodded. "Well, we accept that as tender here. Our ship's account will, of course, have to verify those once we reach your vessel. If she is not satisfied, we will drop you off, and your deposit will be forfeit. Is that agreeable?"

"Of course," Katrina replied. "I don't anticipate any issues."

"Excellent."

The next hour was spent reviewing contracts sent by the firm's NSAI lawyers.

Katrina was surprised that there were no sentient AIs involved in the process. Just Uriah and the NSAIs. Either the woman ranked higher within the company than Katrina suspected, or they trusted the efficacy of their NSAI more than she would have.

In the end the deal was signed, and Katrina's accounts were substantially reduced. She would depart in twelve hours aboard the KSS *Havermere*.

With the agreement finalized, Katrina bid Uriah farewell and walked back out of the KiStar showroom, considering how to spend the next half a day.

It would take an hour to fly the pinnace out to the *Havermere,* and she scheduled a departure time with the

Tsarina dockmaster, who charged her a four-hundred credit fee for early un-racking.

Katrina bit her lip and paid it, noting that she now had less than ten thousand credits in her account.

She wanted nothing more than to find somewhere to sleep and drift off for several hours, but a woman of her supposed station would have to book an expensive room, as well as find a suitable meal. She didn't want to stretch her budget overmuch, so Katrina opted for food. Perhaps afterward, she would go window-shopping to while away the time.

She searched the restaurant listings and found one that served non-vat-grown food; something she had become accustomed to during her years on Victoria.

The restaurant was named 'Tour-Sol' and featured a menu supposedly pulled from various times and places in the history of Sol. There were some staples on the menu that she knew to have been common, and many others that she had never heard of.

Katrina ordered steak tartare, grilling the serving woman on the details of its preparation, and ordered a bottle of wine. Once it arrived and was sampled and poured, she sipped it slowly while observing the other patrons from within her deep hood.

There was little new to learn from such observations. As she had initially expected, Bollam's World was what Luminescent Space in Sirius would have been like if the Noctus had lived amongst the Lumins, rather than been isolated on their mining and manufacturing platforms in orbit of Sirius A.

She supposed it was better in some respects. Here, the underclass could blend in—except for their collars—unlike the Noctus, who had been entirely segregated.

However, the Noctus had developed their own unique cultures and strong social bonds. In Bollam's World, the underclass was always in the presence of the upper class—constantly reminded of their lower social standing or their slavery.

Though the Noctus had been slaves, none had ever worn a collar. Both societies were repugnant, but Katrina couldn't make a judgement as to which was worse.

Her meal, which was prepared to perfection, arrived, and she ate it daintily. Afterward, she poured another glass of wine and drank it slowly while researching other star systems along the *Intrepid*'s most likely trajectory.

New Eden was rimward of Kapteyn's Star, and Bollam's World lay beyond it. Although Kapteyn's Streamer continued for some distance beyond Bollam's World, it grew progressively more diffuse, until it dissipated near the Pleiades.

Katrina summoned a holo projection that only she could see, and placed a three dimensional grid around the stars near the Streamer. There were over three hundred. Even with FTL, it would take her years to search all those systems.

Another possibility, she realized, *is that the* Intrepid *exited the Streamer deep in interstellar space, and realized that there were no uncolonized stars anywhere nearby.*

Would they have proceeded without visiting any colonized systems? The edge of human expansion was over three thousand light years away. It would take the *Intrepid* ten thousand years to reach that fringe. It would be too slow; by the time they reached the edge of known space, humanity would have spread further.

No, the *Intrepid* would have to settle somewhere nearby. Or secure FTL capabilities of its own.

Katrina finished her wine and paid for the food, tipping the serving woman well. It was the least she could do for these people.

As she 'walked' back into the corridor outside the restaurant, she realized how sore her ankles had become from staying en point for so long. The boots offered no flexibility, and she was determined to find somewhere out of the way to remove the footwear and stretch her ankles.

"Crap," Katrina whispered.

Somehow, it had not occurred to her that she would be spending three days aboard the KSS *Havermere* on the way back to the *Voyager*. A woman in her position would not wear the same outfit each day—even one as fantastic as this. Maintaining the fiction of her high-class status was imperative for her plan to succeed.

Katrina suffered her sore ankles for awhile longer and returned to the upscale shopping district to spend more of her diminishing credit on expanding her wardrobe.

The selection on her decreased budget was slimmer, and she was forced to buy several of the more common, garish skinsheaths—although she did splurge on a pair of gleaming red boots that would allow her feet to touch the ground, yet still complement Verisa's favorite outfit.

Once her shopping trip was complete, Katrina returned to the docks, a case with her purchases floating through the air behind her.

She found an upscale bar that catered to travelers—something she ascertained by the type of clothing, and lack of visible mods—and settled onto one of the plush barstools, pushing the one to her right out of place to make room for her floating case.

Once her drink was ordered, Katrina pulled the a-grav boots off and placed them in the case. A brief internal debate followed as to whether or not she should put on the new red boots. In the end, the desire for comfort won, and Katrina hooked her unshod feet on the barstool and sipped the martini that was set before her.

She gave the bartender—another human—a curt nod of thanks for the drink. The number of humans performing everyday tasks on the station was quite surprising. Katrina supposed that was what happened when you kidnapped the passengers of every ship that dumped out of the Streamer: lots of excess labor.

As the bartender moved aside, Katrina caught sight of herself in the mirror. Her hood had slipped back partway, and her hair sparkled and flared, making it appear as though her face was wreathed in fire. Each time she took a sip of her drink, the 'cutout' on her chest showed molten gouts of fire flowing past. She looked like a vision from someone's nightmares—or perhaps dreams.

She twisted her lips into a wicked smile, finding it hard not to fall into the Verisa persona when seeing herself like this. Then a thought of Laura came into her mind; the young lady who had only ever known Katrina as a sedate elder stateswoman.

Katrina didn't know whether to give a haughty laugh or drown herself in her drink.

Being Verisa was exhausting. Perhaps she could just be Katrina for these last few hours before boarding the *Havermere*.

*****

Juasa had followed KiStar's newest client from the Tour-Sol restaurant to Lourmis Boulevard, where she had taken only an hour to buy what looked like a half-dozen outfits—probably a record for a woman of her stature.

From there, the woman had wandered down the sweep outside the dock entrances until she came to Gregor's—one of the nicer bars on this side of Tsarina station.

Tommy had said her name was Verisa. It was an interesting name, and not one that Juasa had heard before; somehow it suited the tall, sure woman.

It was hard for Juasa not to stare. Verisa had a perfect figure—albeit one that was almost impossible to properly make out under the amazing skinsheath she wore. If Juasa didn't know better, she'd think that Verisa's body was *actually* made of fire wrapped in writhing black strips of gleaming cloth.

Though the outfit made Verisa look more than a little intimidating, Juasa found it to be a refreshing change from most of the garish outfits that the station's elite preferred.

Juasa had been following Verisa for some time, but she had still not seen the woman's face. She wondered what it would be like. *Would her features be soft, aquiline? Would she have full lips, or would they be drawn and thin, disapproving of everything the haughty woman saw?*

Juasa was certain that she'd seen a curl of red hair from beneath the hood. It would match the skinsheath beautifully. She wondered if the woman's skin was light or dark. Dark would be so deliciously in line with the suit's malicious look, like she was a demon of smoke and fire. Light, however, would make her appear ethereal, like a wraith.

The woman she watched settled on her barstool, and moved one of the other stools out of the way to make room for her hovering case of clothing.

Just like an elite; no concern for others, just their own comfort.

Juasa leaned against an empty table next to the door and watched as Verisa ordered a drink, and then proceeded to pull off her a-grav boots. Juasa didn't blame her; spending hours with one's feet held en pointe was probably rather uncomfortable—though the position had made Verisa's thighs and ass look amazing as she had glided through the station.

Don't be stupid, Juasa, she cautioned herself. *When you approach her, your eyes never leave her face. Keep your tongue in your mouth.*

Then the woman did something that made Juasa wonder about all her previous assessments.

After removing the a-grav boots, she didn't put on any other footwear. Instead, Verisa gave a little smirk and wiggled her toes before hooking her feet on the barstool and picking up her martini for another sip.

Somehow, with that simple action, Verisa had changed. She appeared softer, more forgiving and approachable.

Maybe she's not queen bitch.

Then Verisa pulled down her large hood, and long red hair that curled slightly at the ends fell down around her shoulders.

Juasa's breath caught in her throat; the woman was a goddess, so beautiful it made her heart ache. Verisa's skin was pale, and her green eyes surveyed the bar with a sharp intensity.

She noted that Verisa did not seem to have the agelessly youthful look caused by multiple rejuv visits, but instead appeared to be slightly older than normal—she even had small wrinkles around her eyes.

It was uncommon to see an elite look so…human—especially given the image her clothing projected.

Juasa knew that Tommy must have been wrong. There was no way this woman could be a heartless bitch. Juasa prayed that if she asked nicely, and maybe offered something in return, perhaps she could convince Verisa to help her out of the bind she was in.

Even if she declined, the opportunity to spend some time in such a woman's company would be well worth it.

She took a deep breath and promised herself that she would behave as naturally as possible; *they always said to 'be yourself', right?*

Her foot didn't want to move at first, but once she took the first step, it got easier. Before she knew it, Juasa was walking across the floor to sit at the woman's side.

*****

The bar was warm, and Katrina let down her hood, shaking out her long red hair and letting it cascade over her shoulders. She took another sip of the martini, and was staring down at the streaks of fire tracing across her hands when a woman sat on the stool to her left.

Katrina didn't have to give more than glance out of the corner of her eye to see that it was a KiStar employee, glowing softly in her white uniform with its purple and blue logo—just one though; no mobile display here.

She was young, appearing to be thirty or so—real years. There were no signs of the too-perfect skin that rejuv often caused. Her skin was a pleasant light brown, her face framed by long dark hair.

"Fashion can be a bitch," the woman said with a nervous smile and a nod to Katrina's feet before she held up a hand to signal the bartender.

The woman must have been referring to Katrina's unshod feet—she had to have been watching her for a few minutes, to see her remove the a-grav boots.

Katrina arched an eyebrow. "At times, but it's always worth it. A wise man once said, 'clothing makes the man'—or woman, in my case."

The woman laughed. "I wouldn't know. Well, I should say that I barely remember. KiStar likes us to always be in their colors. Gets a bit boring, but it cuts down on shopping trips."

"Can I help you with something?" Katrina asked, keeping her tone neutral. It was no coincidence that a KiStar employee had shown up here and initiated a conversation.

The woman gave a nervous laugh. "Um, oh, sorry, I forgot to introduce myself. My name is Juasa. I'm Crew Chief aboard the *Havermere*. I'll be the one working on your ship."

"Verisa," Katrina said and offered her hand, which Juasa cautiously reached for and shook only once before pulling her hand back. It was as though she were afraid the angry glow tracing itself across Katrina's skin would burn her.

"I would have expected you to be making preparations aboard the *Havermere*." Katrina asked, wondering when the woman would ask what she had come to ask—whatever that was.

Juasa twisted her lips and gave a rueful laugh. "Yeah, I really should be. I came onstation yesterday 'cause I had a few days off, but looks like that's been cut short."

"Sorry to inconvenience you," Katrina said, though her tone conveyed no apology.

Juasa ignored Katrina's undertones and waved her hand with a dismissive expression. "Not your fault. Uriah's peeved at me. I gave a client a discount a few months back, and now she does her best to pull me off break whenever possible. Your job probably made her day."

"So why is it that we're sharing a drink here?" Katrina asked, allowing a slight smile. Juasa's honesty and buoyant attitude were a nice change from most of the people Katrina had met on Tsarina.

The bartender set a drink in front of Juasa, and she took a sip. Either she'd passed her preference to the man over the Link, or she was a regular. Or both.

"Tommy—the guy you didn't want to talk to at our sales office, told me about you. Then I talked to a friend I have in station security to see if he could spot you. He pointed me to Tour-Sol, and I followed you from there."

Katrina nodded slowly. Keeping a low profile hadn't been in her plan, though she didn't expect it to garner her this sort of visit, either.

"Why are you dissembling, Juasa?" Katrina asked. "I asked why you're here, not how you found me."

Juasa made a clicking sound with her cheek and turned slightly, her posture more open and vulnerable. "It's a bit embarrassing, really. Captain Ferris is pissed at me—more than usual. He was about to disembark and have a good couple of days with some of his lady friends onstation, when the call came in that we were going back out. He knows Uriah has her shiny blue hair in a twist about me, and that's why our whole ship's leave got cut short—again."

"Still waiting for why you're here," Katrina said, holding back a smile. There was something about Juasa that she found herself liking. Here Katrina sat, playing the Verisa cold fish attitude—though a bit softer than she probably should be, perhaps due to the martini—and Juasa hadn't adjusted her behavior one iota.

The woman wasn't dumb; Katrina could see a bright wit and sharp mind behind the hazel eyes. Juasa simply seemed uninterested in playing the class game.

Juasa winked before replying. "Well, the captain recalled our shuttle. Told me I'll have to hop a dockcab to get out to the ship. Problem is, I just paid for three days at a spa, and they don't give refunds for short cancellations, so..."

"Sounds like KiStar has some personnel issues they need to deal with," Katrina said. "Who is Uriah, anyway, that she can make a mess like this?"

Juasa gave a rueful laugh. "She's the owner's daughter. Likes to think she runs the place."

"The owner's daughter runs sales out of the showroom?" Katrina asked and then gestured at Juasa's uniform. "I'm surprised that she wears the same outfit as the rank and file."

"Her father makes her. I think he's trying to teach her humility. It doesn't bother me; some good things have come out of her working the floor."

"What might those be?" Katrina asked before taking a sip of her martini, wondering at this woman who was sharing all of this information so freely. *What are her intentions? Or maybe she is just an open book type of person*.

Juasa grinned and continued. "Well, for starters, the old uniforms used to be a weird muddy brown and purple. Uriah wouldn't stand for that, and got us this much nicer design."

Katrina chuckled. "At least she's good for something."

Juasa nodded slowly. "She's actually good at her job. I mean…it's all she has now, and she's managed that transition well enough."

"All she has?" Katrina asked.

"Oh, you didn't notice," Juasa pulled her skinsheath away from her neck. My uniform comes off. Hers doesn't. She even blushes blue and purple."

Katrina shook her head and laughed. "I'd noticed that. You're saying that her skin is her uniform, or something like it?"

"Yup," Juasa nodded. "Her dad thought she was a flighty little dumbass—which wasn't far from the truth. Anyway, he told her how she had to prove that she's KiStar through and through. He meant it literally. That's been her skin for six years now. She still has another nineteen to go."

"Then what?" Katrina asked, setting her empty martini glass down and signaling for another.

"Put it on my tab," Juasa said to the man as he walked past.

Katrina didn't know if she should accept, but given the state of her account, she'd take the generosity.

"Where was I? Oh, right. So, she wears the company uniform for twenty-five years, purple eyes, lips, the whole deal. Now, mind you, she can go and get her pink and fleshy skin back whenever she wants. But if she does, she's disinherited. But if she pisses blue, white, and purple for the full twenty-five, he gives her KiStar."

Katrina snorted. "Seems like a strange ritual to force on her to get her inheritance. The ability to wear clothes doesn't mean she can run a company."

Juasa nodded. "Yeah, there are some other stipulations in there about sales and whatnot, but you don't know how Uriah used to be. She had a different outfit for every hour of the day. She modded herself six ways from Sunday every other week. That girl has had horns, a tail, tails for horns, flippers, a shark fin; if you can dream it, she's turned herself into it. Her father made her sacrifice all of that for the chance to run KiStar."

"When you put it that way, I can imagine that it has been a disciplining experience for her."

"You can say that again. I didn't think she'd last a week. Needless to say, I'll never see those hundred creds I put into the 'quitting pool' again." Juasa leaned in and held a hand to the side of her mouth. "Now we all call her the White Queen—but not to her face, of course."

Juasa's casual and friendly banter was infectious. Even though she had obviously shown up just to mooch a ride to her ship, the woman seemed genuine and sincere—either that, or she was a consummate actor.

Katrina supposed that *was* possible. It could be that every word out of her mouth was a lie, and she was just having some fun at the expense of a new client.

But that didn't seem like a wise career move—though, airing your company's dirty laundry didn't seem smart, either; even if it did make Uriah seem a bit more relatable.

At the very least, it explained why Uriah had negotiated the terms with Katrina on her own. She was far from being a lowly salesperson—sort of.

Either way, it was nice to have someone talk to her like she was nobody special—someone other than Troy. It had been a long time since Katrina had engaged in casual banter.

She accepted her new martini from the bartender and raised it to Juasa before taking a sip.

Juasa raised hers as well, a slight smile on her soft lips. As they had talked, the young woman had turned on her seat to face Katrina full-on. There was nothing guarded about her posture, no tells that she was hiding anything.

It fact, it was quite the opposite. Juasa's gaze had mostly stayed on Katrina's face as they'd spoken—mostly on her eyes, but often on her lips as well.

Once or twice, Juasa had even made a gesture like she was going to touch Katrina's arm, but pulled back at the last minute.

As they spoke, something had happened to Katrina, too; something that she had not felt in a long, long time. So long that she had forgotten all about it.

It was a quickening of her heart when Juasa met her eyes, when the young girl smiled, when she raised her arms to gesticulate as she spoke.

Am I lusting after this young woman? Katrina wondered. She knew what Verisa would do. The aristocrat would take Juasa onto her pinnace, and take what pleasures she wished from the eager young woman.

She tried to tell herself that it was for the cover; that wooing the crew chief on the ship was a good move, and would help with the subterfuge she would have to employ. But as the delicious sensations of her blood pressure rising and her breath quickening flowed through her, she found that she didn't care.

Katrina reached out and placed a hand on Juasa's knee while a smile danced on her sparkling red lips. "And when would you like me to give you a ride to the *Havermere*?"

Juasa placed her hand over Katrina's, and the understanding in her eyes was plain to see. "Thanks for not making me ask; you're a very gracious woman, Verisa—even if I was certain you'd be a she-devil when I first saw you. I'm still surprised that you don't have horns to go with that outfit."

Katrina barked a laugh at Juasa's continued audacity, and gave her a haughty glare that Juasa grinned at before asking, "How does 'as soon as you're done with that drink' sound?"

HAVERMERE

STELLAR DATE: 11.14.8511 (Adjusted Gregorian)
LOCATION: Bay 1342, Tsarina Commerce District #3 (station)
REGION: Tsarina, Bollam's World System (58 Eridani)

"This is *nice,*" Juasa said as she settled into the copilot's seat in the pinnace's cockpit. "So clean too, like it's new."

"I like to keep things tidy," Katrina replied as she pulled her harness on.

"You expecting something I don't know about?" Juasa asked as she eyed Katrina's harness.

Katrina bit back a curse. She had hoped that, in this world, a small craft like her pinnace didn't normally have artificial gravity systems; now she saw that it had been a fool's hope.

"No a-grav in here," Katrina replied casually as she lowered the pinnace's canopy.

"Well, that's weird," Juasa scowled as she pulled on her harness. "Top of the line skiff like this…you'd think it would have all the bells and whistles."

"It's retro," Katrina said as she ran the pre-flight checks. She was slowly adjusting her speech patterns to match Juasa's. Making the woman feel comfortable around her was key to success. "I like zero-*g*, so I never bothered to get it upgraded."

Juasa was giving Katrina a curious look. Then she laughed and shook her head. "You're a strange she-devil, that's for sure. Aren't you worried about atmo leaks, or flying around without a shield? A stray pebble, and you and I are both sucking vacuum."

"What does a devil have to worry about such things for?" Katrina said with a laugh. "Seriously, though; the ship has ES shields capable of holding atmosphere, should we blow a seal."

"ES…as in electrostatic?" Juasa sputtered.

"Yes, do you still want a ride?" Katrina said with a smirk and a raised eyebrow.

"Uh…yeah, I guess. You weren't kidding about this being old school, though. I've only seen a few ES emitters. I'd love to have a look at yours when we dock on the *Havermere*.

"Perhaps," Katrina said. "We're green for liftoff—they'll shoot us out any moment now.

Juasa just barely finished fastening her harness before the pinnace rose above the cradle on an antigravity column, and shot out of the bay.

"Holeee shitting stars!" Juasa exclaimed. "Er…sorry about that…I don't often get to feel raw *g*s like that."

"It was only three," Katrina replied. "And don't worry about the language. I'm not as uptight as I was putting on back onstation."

"We'll that's good," Juasa said. "Stars, was I ever nervous about hitting you up for a ride—especially after I saw you. Where did you get that outfit, anyway? I've never seen anything like it."

"I got it on Lourmis Boulevard."

"No…no one on station sells anything like that."

Katrina laughed as she remembered the struggle she had with the salesperson. "Well, it was supposed to hint at a beautiful meadow through what looked like pink ribbons, but the forced perception was off; it couldn't do the distance properly. I was having trouble finding anything to taste, when I saw it glitch and I wondered if it could show something simpler."

"So you picked a hellscape?" Juasa asked with a laugh.

Katrina shrugged. "It was the best thing that they had. The flames are all indistinct and right at the surface, so the forced perspective issues aren't as hard to deal with. Either way, he was glad to finally sell it, I think, so when we agreed on the software patch, he was more than happy to do it and get it, and me, out of his store."

"I wonder if you'll start a new trend on the station," Juasa mused. "I could stare at it all day."

"I've noticed," Katrina replied with a smirk, then shook her head. The alcohol and her emotions were blurring the lines between Katrina and Verisa. She could use her internal mednano to clear out the booze and normalize her hormones, but where would the fun be in that? What she was feeling…it felt too good to stop. A little lessening of the inhibitions may be just what she needed right then.

"I have the *Havermere* on scan," Katrina said as the pinnace's sensors picked up their destination. "Looks like it will only take us about forty minutes to get out there."

They had cleared the station's no-thrust zone, and Katrina brought up the chem boosters. The pinnace leapt forward, and Katrina set it on a course for the *Havermere* before shutting the drives down and letting the ship drift through the traffic around the Tsarina Station.

Juasa whistled. "You fly manual, too? With chem boosters? You're quite the enigma. You're lucky traffic is light. Dockmaster would be up your ass for using chems so close to Tsarina, otherwise."

Katrina reached over and placed her hand high on Juasa's thigh. "Don't worry, Juasa. I only like to live a little dangerously. Unless you can't handle that."

Juasa smiled and placed her hand on top of Katrina's. "I can handle it all right. They have NSAI where this thing's from, right? It can autopilot?"

Katrina nodded and her eyes narrowed hungrily. "Yes, yes, it can. There's a small cabin in the back. I think it's time you paid me for giving you a lift.

*****

If there was one thing that Katrina had learned over her decades of operating as a spy for the Lumins, it had been compartmentalization. She had also leveraged those skills after Markus's death, during her time as President of Victoria, and again during the search for the *Intrepid*.

Never before had she been so thankful for the skill.

Not just because she needed to tuck away the betrayal she felt to Markus, but because she honestly needed the release.

A release that Juasa was well-able to provide. The woman was adept both with her fingers and her mouth. For someone who worked with their hands for a living, hers were surprisingly smooth, and the nails on the ends of her delightful fingers were thankfully short.

Katrina had returned pleasure for pleasure, bringing Juasa to orgasm more than once, ensuring that the thought of more would constantly be on Juasa's mind.

They had careened across the cabin, pushing off the deck, the walls, and the overhead, eventually losing all sense of direction—only intent on one another's bodies.

By some miracle, they had eventually found their way back to the bunk, above which both women now floated; chests heaving, arms and legs entangled, and a sheen of sweat glistening on their skin.

"I have to admit," Juasa said, her voice soft and almost timid. "I thought you'd be stiff, demanding. But damn, Verisa, you know how to give a good time."

"I've been around," Katrina replied. "Learned a few things here and there."

Juasa smirked. "Just a few? Seems like you're a living database of just the right moves."

Katrina twisted to the side and looked down at Juasa's flat stomach and the EVA sustenance port that stood out from where her navel should be. She reached out and traced a finger around it, causing Juasa to giggle.

"Stop it! I told you that tickles," Juasa said with a snort.

"Sorry," Katrina said, wrinkling her nose a smidge. "I'm just wondering about what you have to go through for your work. You and I live such different lives…. You must spend a lot of time in the black to have one of these."

Juasa sighed. "Sometimes, yeah. Done my share of multi-day stints in the black before. The paste that KiStar loads the EVA suits with is pretty gross." She patted the port. "This little mod means I don't have to taste that shit."

"Maybe someday you'll be free from all this," Katrina said as she grabbed a strap and pulled them back down to the bed.

Katrina was surprised that she'd uttered the words aloud. The thought of offering Juasa a ride out of Bollam had occurred to her as she made love to the woman.

It shouldn't have; her quest didn't have room for hitchhikers, but as she gazed at Juasa's smile, she couldn't help but be enamored of such a free spirit.

That she should be shackled to a stratified oligarchy like that of Bollam's World was the height of misfortune.

Well—not the height, but it was up there.

"Yeah, right," Juasa said. "Take a miracle for me to get out of this system."

Katrina swung a leg out and hooked it into a strap on the cabin's floor, swinging herself up and stretching to reach one of the hooks on the overhead. She gasped in surprise as Juasa's fingers slid up between her legs, causing her to let out a long moan of pleasure.

There may be an ancillary reason why I wouldn't mind having Juasa come away with me….

She turned and looked down at the dark-haired woman, her lithe body stretched seductively and now resting against the bunk, pushed down into it from the motion of sliding her hand into Katrina.

Juasa pulled her fingers out and gently stroked Katrina's thighs before pulling her hand back.

"You're such a tease, Juasa," Katrina said with unfaked longing in her voice.

Juasa sucked on the fingers that had just been inside Katrina's body, and gave a coy smirk. "I know."

Katrina turned and bent over Juasa, smelling her own scent on the other woman's lips before giving her a passionate kiss—which she abruptly cut off. "Two can play at that game," Katrina said as she pushed off and drifted toward the san unit, posing seductively as she floated away.

"Oh stars, I'm so glad it'll take three days 'til we get to your ship," Juasa said from the bunk.

Five minutes later, Juasa was in the san, moaning in delight at the luxury of a water shower on such a small pinnace. Katrina had to admit that she was surprised to find a water shower as well, but wasn't going to question the provenance.

She shimmied into a green skinsheath that sported shifting red and gold highlights—the red a perfect match for her hair—and pulled up the fastener, which then all but disappeared into the outfit.

She gave a shake of her head to reset her hair, and Katrina knew she would knock the socks off her next target, Captain Ferris. From what she had learned of him from a few brief queries—plus Juasa's comments—she would need to get him to play along with her scheme to trade stasis pods for tech.

He also appeared to have two weakness: a desire to elevate himself to a higher station, and women. Luckily for Katrina, she embodied both of those desires in one person.

Before she made her way back out to the cockpit, she leaned over Juasa's KiStar uniform and touched the inside of her lapel, depositing a dose of nano onto it.

The tiny robots would seed themselves within the uniform and provide a backup to the nano she had already inserted inside Juasa. With the limited nanotech at Juasa's disposal, the young woman's body would never even know it had been infiltrated.

Once the nano had done its job, Katrina would be privy to everything Juasa did, and have access to all her Link communications.

It felt like a betrayal, and she didn't do it lightly—but even though the tryst with Juasa had felt amazing, Katrina still had a mission and a ship to keep safe out in the far reaches of the system.

She set aside her reservations and confirmed that the nano had properly settled in. That task complete, Katrina slipped on the red, non-hovering boots, and pulled herself through the cabin's door and back into the cockpit.

Ahead, the *Havermere* was just a small dot, and Katrina flicked a hand at the holoscreen, causing the display to zoom in and enlarge the ship.

The *Havermere* certainly appeared cut out for the job required. It consisted of a kilometer-long hull, which sported three-hundred-meter armatures at regular intervals. Mounted atop the body were large tanks and cargo pods; several spare pieces of hull were even strapped to its side with cargo netting. It was the epitome of a ship built for function over form.

Katrina pulled on her harness and sent a ping to the ship while she listened to Juasa getting dressed in the cabin behind her.

"I've signaled them," she said over her shoulder.

"They'll send you to a dock near the bow," Juasa said as she floated into the cockpit and reached out to touch the holoscreen. "Here."

"And so they have," Katrina replied as the response came back. "It seems Captain Ferris sends his regards, and is glad you found a ride."

Juasa snorted. "He better be glad. He may be a half-decent captain—when his ego and aspirations aren't making him act like a flaming asshole—but he doesn't have the first clue about repairing ships."

"What about sleeping with clients," Katrina asked. "What does he think about that?"

Juasa laughed, a soft bubbling sound of contentment. "I recall no sleeping."

"Seriously," Katrina said, hardening her aristocratic persona's voice. "Will he call your judgement into question?"

"No," Juasa snorted. "He'll be jealous."

Katrina laughed aloud, though inwardly she felt sorry for Juasa. This young woman was going to get hurt in the next few days. When all was said and done, she may not *want* to leave Bollam's World, at least not with Katrina. Which was probably for the best anyway. Katrina's mission was one of singular focus; not a joyride across the stars.

Katrina decided that now would be a good time to gauge Juasa's reaction to rejection. "Perhaps it would be wise if we kept this tryst to ourselves."

Sure enough, Juasa's face fell. Whatever had happened between them had meant more to the crew chief than just some short fling to say thank you for a ride.

It was going to make what would happen aboard the *Havermere* even more painful.

Maybe there's a way around this…

"Juasa, I have something to tell you…I haven't been completely honest," Katrina began, watching Juasa's expression grow even more worried. "I'm not some wealthy upper-crust aristocrat—at least, not yet, anyway. I'm completely broke. I have no money."

Juasa's eyes widened; as Katrina suspected, that was not the revelation the woman had expected to hear.

"But…you have money, you bought all those clothes…"

Katrina shrugged. "I had to make Uriah think I had the money to pay for the repairs, which I don't. I do, however, have tech that I can trade for them."

Juasa's eyes narrowed. "Ferris doesn't like deals with trades, it can get messy—especially since you didn't tell Uriah about that."

"It's because of what the tech is. It's Streamer tech."

Juasa sat back in her seat and shook her head. "Now it's real messy. What is it?"

"Stasis pods," Katrina replied simply.

Juasa let out a long whistle. "Well that takes the cake. I've seen a lot of interesting stuff come out of the Streamer, but never stasis pods…. Do they work?"

Katrina nodded. "Yup, I've used one."

"Shiiiiiit, this is next-level crazy, Verisa. Dammit…." Juasa shook her head. "Just one stasis pod is probably enough to pay for everything—how many do you have?"

"Ten," Katrina lied.

Juasa rubbed her hands across her face and through her hair. "Ferris is going to have trouble with this. He may claim your ship as Streamer salvage; KiStar has rights for that, you know."

"'Streamer salvage'?" Katrina asked. Whatever that was, it was something she'd missed in her research.

Juasa chuckled. "A little set of laws that pretty much legalizes piracy here. Ships with SS rights can seize any ship coming out of the Streamer, and its tech. The burden of proof required to show that a ship actually *did* come out of the Streamer is pretty light, too. Your ten pods are more than enough for Ferris to lay claim to your ship—and you."

That was just the outcome that Katrina feared, but she still had to deal with it. Getting the *Voyager* FTL-capable was imperative, and having a repair ship out with her in the black to do it was still better than coming into a station.

"So what are Ferris's weaknesses?" Katrina asked. She knew the answer, but she wanted this to be Juasa's idea.

Juasa's eyes darted down, her gaze raking across Katrina's body. "He wants to rise above his current station; he craves the idea of moving in more aristocratic circles. You would be a prime example of what he desires."

"Are you suggesting what I think you are?" Katrina asked tentatively.

Juasa looked away and stared off into space for a minute before turning back to Katrina. "Stupid, right? We just met a few hours ago, but I feel like something clicked with us, Verisa. I'm not keen on sharing you for these few days we'll have, but things won't go well for you if we don't do something…."

Katrina locked eyes with Juasa. "Something like me seducing Captain Ferris."

"Yeah, like that."

"Would it even work?" Katrina asked. "Would sleeping with him be enough to convince him not to turn me in, and maybe to get him to take a pod in trade?"

"Not on its own, no. You'll have to persuade him. I'm not sure how, to be honest."

Katrina nodded silently. She would have to work something out. Or simply take control of the *Haveremere*. With Juasa's help, she didn't anticipate that such a task would be too difficult; though it might be messy. That was, if she could convince the woman to turn on her own people.

A small voice in Katrina's mind made the point that she was on a fool's errand. It wasn't as though the *Intrepid* really needed her help. This mission was about her, not them. *Can I really disrupt these people's lives in my own quest to find my friends?*

Well, I didn't choose to land here, in a system populated by thieves. I have a right to defend what's mine.

A hand touched her arm, and Katrina turned to see Juasa looking at her intently.

"You do what you need to do, Katrina. I don't want to see you hurt."

Katrina placed her hand over Juasa's. "Nor you. I have a plan forming. You're going to have to trust me. In the end, I'll make sure you're safe."

*****

"My lady Verisa," Captain Ferris said as Katrina stepped out of the pinnace, floating down the ramp on her a-grav boots—which Juasa had insisted she wear. She counseled that they would impress Ferris and add to his belief in her elevated social stature.

Katrina stopped before the captain and gave him a neutral smile while inclining her head. "Captain Ferris, I thank you for allowing me to come aboard your ship. I was not anticipating another long ride alone in my pinnace."

Ferris appeared exactly as his personnel records had shown. He stood well over two meters tall—the child of generations of spacers—and his skin was almost translucently pale, as though his body produced no melanin whatsoever. However, his long blonde hair and pale blue eyes suited his coloring, and complimented the KiStar uniform well.

"Of course, of course," Ferris replied as he offered his hand. "It is a pleasure to have you aboard the *Havermere*."

Katrina placed her hand out, palm down, and Ferris awkwardly shook it. She sighed with thinly veiled disdain. "I trust you have suitable quarters for me?" she asked.

"Of course, of course," Ferris replied and then looked up at Juasa. "Ju, get the lady's bags and bring them to her quarters."

"And where would those be?" Juasa asked dryly.

Ferris gave her a cold look. "Next to mine, of course."

Katrina was surprised to see Ferris behave so dismissively toward Juasa given the docking bay crews within earshot. From what she understood of the structure on a KiStar repair ship, Ferris didn't exactly outrank Juasa. The animosity he just displayed would not be good for cohesion between the repair crews and the ship's crew.

<*Sorry,*> she said to Juasa over the Link—her first time speaking with the woman nonverbally.

<*I'm used to it,*> Juasa replied.

<*Shouldn't have to be, though.*>

"You're very lucky that the *Havermere* was available," Captain Ferris said as he led Katrina out of the bay and into a utilitarian passageway. "We're one of the most well-equipped ships in the KiStar fleet. Handling jobs like yours is our specialty. Just last month, we re-fitted a seven-klick ore hauler to have FTL capability. Its owners wanted to start selling our volatiles into other systems. It only took us nine days to get that ship ready to make its first jump."

"That's very impressive timing," Katrina replied. "Do you expect to have things done that quickly with my ship?"

She knew it was more a question for Juasa, but the goal was to give Ferris the opportunity to feel important; something he seemed all too eager to do.

"Oh, we'll have to see. I imagine a lady such as yourself has a much more refined vessel than some ore hauler. With a ship like that, we can bolt grav systems right on the hull. If your lines are any indication of your ship's, we'll want to be more discrete."

<*Oh, brother,*> Juasa commented privately from her place behind the pair.

<I wouldn't have minded it coming from you,> Katrina replied. *<For some reason it's just creepy coming from him.>*

<Probably because he's a creep.>

Aloud, Katrina laughed softly, giving Ferris a confidence boost. "The *Voyager* is indeed a ship of singular beauty. I'm not interested in any work that will mar her appearance."

"I should expect not," Ferris said, pausing at a lift entrance and gesturing for Katrina to enter first. Juasa followed, giving Ferris a sickly sweet smile as she did so.

Ferris fought back a scowl, and waited for Katrina's luggage to tag along on its floats before entering the lift.

<Juasa, he is completely into you,> Katrina said.

<What? No, he hates me,> Juasa replied.

<Apparently you can't see the galaxy for the stars here, Juasa. At some point you've rejected this man, and he's still taking it out on you.>

<Huh,> was all Juasa said.

Katrina imagined Juasa was trying to determine when that was. Based on how attractive Juasa was, and Ferris's general demeanor, Katrina suspected the moment of rejection was at their first meeting.

"You'll be on the executive deck," Ferris said as the lift rose. "Our ship's AI will ensure you have all access to schedules and feeds. I would, of course, be delighted if you'd join us in the officers' mess for meals."

"Of course," Katrina said. "I trust that your cooks are capable of preparing suitable meals?"

A look of worry crossed Ferris's face, and he glanced at Juasa as though he hoped she would tell him Katrina's favorite dish. "Uhmm, of course, we have an extensive menu."

<Yeah, when oceans fly,> Juasa said with a mental chuckle.

Katrina placed a hand on Ferris's arm. "Excellent, I look forward to sampling what you have to offer."

She felt Ferris stiffen beneath her touch, then the lift's doors opened and he stepped out into the passageway. "Of course. Your cabin is this way."

He led Katrina down a corridor that was less utilitarian, but still far from ornate. Plain white bulkheads were painted with blue and purple stripes in the KiStar colors. The lighting was muted enough that the white bulkheads weren't glaring, but the plain coloring wasn't particularly welcoming either.

Katrina did have an errant thought of all the KiStar employees blending into the corridors with their matching uniforms, and bumping into one another repeatedly.

Ferris stopped at one of the doors, which opened silently.

"Your quarters for the duration of our trip," he said, gesturing within.

Katrina swept past him and took stock of the cabin. It was large for a ship like the *Havermere,* but at just five by six meters, not excessively so.

It had a wide bed, drawers built into one of the bulkheads, and a table and desk, as well as its own san unit in a corner.

She turned back to the captain and Juasa, who still stood in the corridor, and nodded. "Excellent, captain. This will suffice until I get back on my own ship."

Her cases floated in on the a-grav pad, and Ferris nodded with a wide smile. "I'm glad to hear it. Will you then join us this evening?"

"Perhaps," Katrina replied. "I have spent the day operating on Tsarina's local time, which puts this as the middle of the night."

Ferris flushed and nodded. "Of course; I had forgotten that. No pressure, then."

"Thank you," Katrina said and sent a signal for the door to slide shut.

She settled onto the bed and stared out the porthole into space. In the distance, she could see the bright point of light that was Tsarina station in orbit of the frigid plutino beyond. Just one point of light amongst thousands in the system. Just one system amongst tens of thousands that humans now lived in.

The idea was still mind bogglingly hard for Katrina to adjust to. Less than a week ago—not counting time in stasis—she had been searching for the *Intrepid* in the dark of interstellar space, on the fringe of human expansion. Now, she was deep within the core human worlds.

<*You played him like a harp,*> Juasa said. <*He looked both hurt and terribly expectant as the door shut.*>

<*He makes himself an easy target,*> Katrina replied. <*I will have to join him for the meal; though it has been almost two days since I last slept…*>

<*Of course,*> Juasa said apologetically. <*I'll let you rest. I imagine I sapped some of your reserves with our fun on your skiff.*>

Katrina sent her a smile over the Link. <*Just the opposite. That gave me the energy I needed to go on,*> Katrina replied before pausing and considering her next words carefully. <*You need to be at dinner, and it won't be fun for you. But I'll make it up to you, I promise.*>

<*What do you mean?*> Juasa asked, her mental tone worried.

<*Ferris is going to use me to rub his perceived superiority in your face. I'm probably going to egg him on to do it, and it's going to hurt you. I need you to know that I won't mean a word of it—but that won't change how it feels for you to hear it.*>

Juasa didn't respond for a moment and Katrina suspected that the woman was wondering why she was going through this for Katrina. Or rather, Verisa.

The KiStar crew chief's willingness to suffer through indignities—rather than simply betraying Katrina and taking her share of the bounty that the stasis pods would be sure to bring—would tell Katrina how far she could trust Juasa.

<I don't know why I'm doing this for you, Verisa,> Juasa said. *<Stars, I don't know why I'm being so honest with you, when you're far from transparent….>*

<You and I shared an honesty that cannot be faked,> Katrina replied. *<I give you my oath. Before this is done, I will lay myself bare to you.>*

<Interesting choice of words. I certainly expect to see you laid bare a few more times before we reach your ship,> Juasa grinned over the Link. *<Seriously, though; I'll hold you to that promise. I'll see you at dinner.>*

Katrina sent back a smile and cut the connection.

The bed called to her; it urged her to lay back and let sleep come, but Katrina knew there was too much to do. Her plan with Juasa may work, but she also needed a contingency plan.

Summoning her strength, Katrina rose from the bed and sat down at the desk, activating its holo-controls.

A display rose before her, giving her a menu of options to choose from—everything from basic ship status information, to food and entertainment systems.

Katrina tapped into those, and set a mental subroutine to flipping through those options and previewing the vids and sims. Then she placed a hand on the desk and sent a string of nano into its surface.

The tiny machines slipped through the surface of the desk and into its net interface. She harbored no doubts about the level of access her desk had; it would be locked down and limited in the extreme. However, those protections would all be managed by a software layer.

The desk itself would be wired into the same network matrix that ran other non-critical systems on the ship. And somewhere, that matrix would intersect with the systems that controlled the ship's critical systems.

Once the nano was set on its task of searching out those physical connections—whereupon they would implant themselves in the physical conduit, and sniff the data passing through—Katrina set herself to investigating the ship's AI.

Whether or not it was a true AI was something she needed to determine sooner rather than later. She had seen very few sentient AIs on the nets thus far in the Bollam's World System. Those that she had seen were far from the strong mental presences she was used to when dealing with the AI aboard the *Intrepid,* as well as those who remained behind at Kapteyn's Star.

She reached out to the AI—named Sam—with a query about the ship's recreation facilities, and got a reply back that surprised her.

<Sorry, is there something wrong with your own search abilities? It's right in the menu on your desk.>

The AI's attitude reminded her of Troy, and she felt a smile touch her lips.

<No, the captain indicated that I could speak with you about such matters,> Katrina replied.

<He tends to do that, but I have a lot on my plate. As much as he wants to impress you, I have a ship to run, and since you don't have the detailed specs for your ship handy, Juasa and I are going over all the possible configurations we may have to use. Plus, she has to have a fancy dinner with the rest of you while I keep working, so if you don't mind, I need to make the most of my time with her before that.>

Katrina wanted to laugh and mollify the AI, but that didn't suit her persona.

<I'll kindly ask you to moderate your tone, Sam. I'm paying for this excursion, you know.>

<Great, then let me do my job and get your ship fixed up.>

The AI severed the connection and Katrina knew that she would have to neutralize Sam. With an attitude like that, he was bound to be nosy.

Another task on her to-do list—which already included winning Juasa over to her side and seducing the captain.

She rubbed her hands on her face and sighed. Perhaps once they reached the *Voyager*, Troy could ensure that Sam was kept in check.

*****

Still fresh from her shower aboard the pinnace, and dismayed that her quarters did not have a water san, Katrina forwent the sonic cleaning before changing for dinner with the captain and his officers that evening.

She pulled out the other outfits she had purchased while on Tsarina Station, and considered which would contrast the most with the KiStar uniforms, making her the center of attention. Well, more the center of attention.

One of the skinsheaths was colored a gleaming gold with silver accents that would flow across her body in a mesmerizing fashion, while another was a brilliant pink that shone brightly. It was enhanced by bright blue accents which ran up the inside of the legs, encircled the waist and then wrapped around the breasts before ending on a high collar that rose up behind her head.

Katrina liked the pink outfit, but didn't feel like pulling her hair up in a fashion that would suit the high collar, and opted for the gold outfit.

She slid into it and pulled up the fastener to her neck. Once it reached the top, the skinsheath drew out all the air between itself and her body, making it look like she'd been dipped in gold.

Katrina summoned a holoprojection of herself, and examined the outfit from all sides, to ensure it was perfect. One thing was certain: putting herself on display in such a fashion was the perfect way to hide. She just wished it wasn't so close to the fashions of Luminescent Society.

What I wouldn't give for a long dark jacket.

However, the outfit was just Verisa's style. Katrina added gold ear coverings and adjusted their long, dangling chains, which reached down to her breasts. Next, she applied the golden strips that covered her eyebrows, and then applied red paint to her lips.

Once satisfied that her face was a work of art, Katrina ran a comb through her hair that deposited a powder enhancing its shine, making it glow and sparkle.

Finally, Katrina activated the skinsheath's silver light show. She was certain that it would entice the captain. There was no way he wouldn't be wrapped around her little finger by the end of the night.

She activated the room's holomirror and examined herself from all sides. The image before her was perfection—a gleaming icon of power and confidence. Yet the image's face wore a look of sadness.

Katrina couldn't help but think that she looked like a Lumin, a perfect replica of how her father used to make her mother dress. Even now, thousands of years later, Luminescent Society was still controlling her.

Her displeasure was compounded by the fact that she wanted to be enticing Juasa, not Captain Ferris.

That, in and of itself was a problem. She wondered if—when the time came—she would have the will to use Juasa in whatever manner was necessary to secure the upgrades to the *Voyager* and leave the Bollam's World System.

Hopefully forever.

Katrina pushed those thoughts away, and wrapped herself in Verisa; the persona settling around her like a layer of armor. Her posture straightened, her stance widened, and she threw her shoulders back.

The look of sadness on her face changed into a haughty smile, and she folded her arms across her chest.

"He'll never even know what hit him," she said aloud before dismissing the holomirror with a wave of her hand and striding from the room.

Outside, she followed the trail overlaying her vision to the officers' mess, which was further aft on the same deck. She was already late, but she walked slowly; there was no need for anyone to think she was in a rush.

When she arrived, Katrina swept into the room as though they'd all been awaiting her pleasure—which was probably not far from the truth.

The room's décor was par for the course on the *Havermere*. White with purple and blue accents. The space itself was only six meters square, with a large round table in the center.

Seated around it were Captain Ferris, Juasa, and five other men and women.

Katrina saw that the only empty seat was on the captain's right, and walked toward it as Captain Ferris rose. His gaze happily took in her body long before it met her eyes.

"My lady," he said with a warm smile as he slid out her chair. "I'm glad you have decided to join us."

Katrina inclined her head in acceptance and sat, pulling the chair back in herself.

"Of course, I'm interested in meeting the people who will be working on my ship. That, combined with a meal that you ascertained would please me, ensured my attendance."

<*Holy crap, Verisa, you're so bright I can hardly look at you,*> Juasa commented privately.

<*You sure?*> Katrina asked, passing a lascivious wink over the Link. <*Ferris seems to be having no trouble at all.*>

<*He probably attenuated his vision.*>

"Of course, yes," Ferris said as he resumed his seat. "As I mentioned, I have a top crew."

"Indeed," Katrina said simply as she lifted the glass of white wine at her setting and took a sip.

"On my left is my first mate, Anna," Ferris began by gesturing to the tall, dark-haired woman at his side before continuing clockwise around the table. "Juasa you know already—largely due to her poor planning. Next to her is Carl, her number two, and then Hemry our ship's engineering chief. Tammy is our astronav, and Jan manages the accounts and inventory."

Katrina nodded in turn as Ferris introduced each of the ship's officers, noting the grimace on Juasa's face as Ferris commented on her hitchhiking.

"Very nice to meet you all," Katrina said amicably. Now was the time to begin making Ferris feel that his charm was working on her. She looked over the table, noting that the dinnerware was actually of a high quality, and that the wine glasses were made of blue crystal. "I must say, I was not expecting such class from a repair and refit ship such as the *Havermere*."

Ferris beamed with pride, and Katrina noticed Hemry roll his eyes.

"We do our best," Anna said, her smile less than warm.

Well, she'll be a problem.

"I'm glad to see it," Katrina replied. "Is that real cheese?"

"Of course," Ferris replied. "I always make certain we lay in a good supply. It's the little things that matter."

Katrina met Ferris's eyes. "Yes, yes it is."

"I trust you had a good flight over, and that your quarters are acceptable?" Jan, the ship's financial officer asked.

"Well enough," Katrina said before glancing at Juasa. "Though I was worried first what sort of outfit KiStar was, given the need for me to ferry over your crew chief."

Juasa flushed and pulled at her uniform's cuff, but did not speak.

Ferris, however, shook his head and sighed. "So sorry about that. However, Carl and Juasa make a great team. Now that she's made it to the ship, Juasa's entire focus will be on your upgrades."

Katrina couldn't help but notice the precedence that Ferris gave to Carl over Juasa. The man really was a grade-A asshat. Verisa, however, didn't care and she nodded amicably at Ferris. "Pleased to hear it."

"Can you tell us more about your ship?" Juasa asked, clearly attempting to change the direction of the conversation. "We don't have a lot of information on the Jasepsce Imperial models."

"I provided Uriah with what I had with me," Katrina replied coldly. Surely that is enough to begin your preparations."

A hurt look crossed Juasa's face and her mouth clamped shut.

<Verisa…>

<Hush, Juasa, it's supposed to hurt. Remember what I told you. Ferris wants you. Everything he's doing is to make you feel jealous of him.>

<It just makes me hate him more,> Juasa retorted.

<I didn't say it would work in his favor, just that it's what **he** *thinks will work.>*

<Verisa, I…>

Katrina knew what Juasa was going to say, but it was too soon for that conversation.

<Juasa, please. We just need to get through this right now.>

To her credit, Juasa didn't respond, and Ferris began to talk about the *Havermere's* capabilities, and some of the amazing repairs they had facilitated in the past.

The first course of the meal came as he spoke—a creamy mushroom soup that complemented the wine—and Katrina ate her serving daintily as she listened to the captain.

Some of it was marginally interesting. Several of their repairs had taken place far beyond the heliosphere of the

Bollam's World System. Though Ferris's favorite story was of a time when the *Havermere* had taken control of a Streamer ship.

"There we were, bearing down on them. Their ship had suffered damage coming out of the Streamer, which they do sometimes. The Streamer's shearing forces will tear one ship apart, and not even touch another."

Glad we were in the 'barely touched' category, Katrina thought.

"They had shields though, grav-based, so we knew they had recent tech. Still, any haul is a good haul. We don't have a lot in the way of weapons, but KiStar ensures that we can fend for ourselves. We managed a few well-placed shots, and they lost one of their shield umbrellas. Then we took out their sensor array and punched a hole the hull near the bow."

"I suppose they figured out what was good for them at that point," Katrina said, giving the captain a smile that said she was entirely enamored with his tale of gallantry.

"Indeed they did. They hove to and we boarded them. Turns out that they were a ship from the dark ages, early eighth millennia. No good tech, but some interesting genetic stock. An insystem genetic pharma company bought the lot of them."

Katrina masked her repulsion at the sale of humans, and more notably, at Ferris's casual reference of such. She noticed that Juasa, Tammy, and Hemry also did not appear comfortable with the tale.

Anna, on the other hand laughed. "What a bonus that was. I'd certainly love to find another Streamer ship. Could almost retire if we find another half-decent one."

Katrina took a bite of the salad that had arrived as Anna spoke, and nodded politely. "I should imagine that would be very nice. Mind you, one has to keep an eye out for unexpected expenses…such as this repair."

"What is it that you do?" Ferris asked. "I've been meaning to ask. Your ship looks very impressive; especially for a woman of your stature to be flying alone about the galaxy.

"I'm on my way to Sol," Katrina said with a nonchalant wave of her hand. "I have a buyer there for some tech I managed to acquire out beyond Genevia."

"Out beyond Genevia?" Anna asked, her expression containing no small amount of skepticism. "That's a long way from here. You must have been flying for years to get this far."

Katrina nodded as she took a sip of her wine, and didn't rise to Anna's bait. "Just over two months so far. I like being alone, the company is superb."

Ferris chuckled at her joke while Tammy whistled. "I'd love to see your nav database when we get to your ship. I can only imagine what it would be like to fly out that far."

"Easy now, Tammy," Hemry said. "We all know you dream of taking your skills interstellar someday."

Katrina had noticed that both Carl and Tammy were collared. Tammy had barely spoken during the meal thus far. She suspected that the astronav wasn't flying anywhere outside of Bollam's World so long as that silver band was around her neck.

"To be honest, it's all just more of the same," Katrina said. "Sure there are some weird places out there, but most aren't much different than what you'd find here at Bollam's World."

"I find that hard to believe," Anna said. "Tell us—"

Katrina gave a longsuffering sigh, and Ferris held up his hand. "We've pried into our guest's affairs enough. Look, here comes the main course!"

The main course, as it turned out consisted of a beef-like steak, a baked potato, and a stir fry of various vegetables. It wasn't opulent by any stretch of the imagination, but it tasted good, and Katrina said as much.

"I must admit," Katrina said, placing her hand on Ferris's arm. "I am quite impressed by the quality of your food."

Ferris swallowed a bite and nodded emphatically. "Yusef, our cook, is especially talented. He can make a feast from nearly any supply stock."

Katrina felt a moment of angst. It had been decades since she had heard the name Yusef. And though there was no way this cook was her father, even the thought of that repugnant man was more than she cared to entertain.

<*You OK?*> Juasa asked.

<*Yes, just thinking of something. Don't worry.*>

<*I don't know how you're so calm,*> Juasa said, I'm practically wetting myself over here.

Katrina wished that she could offer Juasa more support. <*I didn't say I'm enjoying it, but so far I've managed to remain calm about it.*>

As they ate, Katrina continued to listen to Ferris talk about himself and the work the ship had done. To hear him tell it, one would think that he single-handedly managed every feat he described.

He also continued to be dismissive toward Juasa, and Katrina noticed that Tammy caught some of his callous comments as well.

The difference between the two was that Tammy had succumbed and slept with Ferris; something that was all to obvious by how Tammy frequently sought Ferris's attention and approval as the night went on.

Katrina couldn't fault the woman. The collar she wore meant that Tammy had virtually no social status beyond her commercial worth; maintaining the favor of her ship's captain was likely of paramount importance to her.

For her part, Katrina laughed at Ferris's jokes—though not all of them—and made certain to touch his arm more than once. That opened the floodgates, and Ferris began to place his hands on her more and more as the meal progressed.

Katrina deftly moved, shifted, and gestured in ways that caused his hand to fall off her body—which wasn't hard, given how smooth her golden sheath was.

However, as the evening progressed, she allowed his touch to linger longer, giving him the impression that he was winning her over.

Once dessert had been served and the officers were enjoying a final drink, he placed a hand on her hip, and Katrina turned slightly, causing it to fall off.

She made a small, soft noise of apology, and reached for his hand, placing it back at the top of her thigh, and pushing his fingers down between her legs.

Ferris's eyes widened, and he quickly downed the last of his drink.

"Verisa," he said with a broad smile. "Would you like to join me for a walk? I can show you around the *Havermere*."

Katrina dabbed a napkin at the corners of her mouth and gave Ferris a long look with half-lidded eyes. "That sounds delightful, lead the way."

Ferris rose from the table and nodded to his officers. "Good evening."

The officers around the table all spoke their farewells, though Juasa barely muttered hers, and only made eye contact with her plate as she did so.

Katrina wanted to reach out to her and remind her that this was all an act, but that would distract her from what was coming with Ferris.

As soon as they were in the corridor, the captain sidled up against Katrina and placed a hand on her ass to guide her.

"I know just the place to start our tour."

It didn't surprise Katrina in the least that the tour began, and ended, in Ferris's quarters.

EXPLANATIONS

STELLAR DATE: 11.15.8511 (Adjusted Gregorian)
LOCATION: KSS *Havermere*, en route to *Voyager*
REGION: Scattered Disk, Bollam's World System (58 Eridani)

The next morning, Katrina waited until the first shift began before leaving her quarters and returning to the officers' mess.

As she'd hoped, it was vacant.

She prepared a bowl of oatmeal and a cup of coffee before sitting at the table with a sigh.

Somehow, thankfully, sleeping with Juasa to win her over had not felt like a betrayal of Markus' memory—at least not in contrast with last night with Ferris. That felt very different.

As the hot coffee washed down her throat, she wondered why that was.

Markus had been gone for a long time—over forty years, give or take a bit. During those years, Katrina had come to believe that she would never fall in love again—and certainly never have sex. She had even fooled herself into believing she didn't miss it.

It would be a lie to say that being with Juasa was not enjoyable. No, not 'enjoyable'; that is doing her a disservice. Juasa was an erotic bout of ecstasy unlike anything I have felt in decades. It is something I'd rather like to repeat.

Ferris had been the opposite. She had pleasured him by rote, using the right techniques at the right time, playing cat and mouse with him, making him crave her.

But there had been no true joining. Not like it had been with Juasa.

Maybe that's why sex with the captain felt like a betrayal.

Markus, if you're out there, watching, or whatever it is you do…I hope you can forgive me. Leaving with you on the Hyperion *was supposed to mark the end of lies and deceit for me.*

How fitting it was that a system descended from Sirius would be the one that would throw her right back into her old ways.

Katrina finished the oatmeal and topped off her coffee before leaving the mess. She wanted to find Juasa, to see that the crew chief was OK.

Katrina reached out to Juasa over the Link, asking where they could meet.

There was no response.

Back in her quarters, Katrina sat at her desk and activated the network bridge her nano had built. They had tapped into one of the ship's maintenance subsystems, and the result was that her usage didn't look like any particular person accessing the network, but rather like an automated system.

If she was careful, it wouldn't throw up any flags.

Katrina used the connection to access the tap she had placed inside Juasa, and found that the woman was in one of the ship's maintenance bays, reviewing the *Havermere*'s stock of graviton emitters.

Juasa's heart rate was elevated, and she had been crying recently.

It felt dirty to spy on Juasa like this. Katrina had hoped that she wouldn't have to use the tap she had placed within the crew chief, but having the woman on her side was more important than anything else right now.

With a few commands, Katrina established a bridge between her personal Link and the desk. Provided that she didn't overuse the bandwidth, it shouldn't raise any suspicions. It would, however, allow her to tap into Juasa—and Captain Ferris, should she need to—whenever she wished.

It took twenty minutes to reach the maintenance bay where Juasa was working. Along the way, Katrina queried a few of the ship's crew as to Juasa's location so that it wouldn't appear as though she just magically knew where to go.

Once she arrived, Katrina stood at the entrance to the bay for some time, watching Juasa as she pulled down a crate and opened it. She reached in and began rummaging through the contents, pulling a few disparate components out and placing them on a nearby bench.

<You're sexy when you're angry,> Katrina said, and then added, *<I kinda like it.>*

It wasn't true; she didn't like it. But what Katrina *had* to say and what she *wanted* to say, were not the same thing.

Juasa spun, her expression one of surprise—but that was fleeting. It only took a moment for anger to darken her features, and then she turned her back to Katrina once more.

<I didn't answer because I didn't want to talk to you.> Juasa's mental tone was clipped, and she slammed the crate's lid closed for emphasis.

<Is this because of what happened at dinner last night, or what happened afterward?>

Katrina stepped inside the maintenance bay and closed the door. Then she tapped the feeds and altered them to make it appear as though the door was still open, supplanting the images and audio with a script she had prepared of she and Juasa discussing the repairs to the *Voyager*.

"You knew this would happen," Katrina said softly as she approached Juasa. "Stars, you proposed it."

Juasa's shoulders slumped and she turned to Katrina with her brow raised high. "I proposed that you sleep with Ferris, yes. I didn't expect you to do it the first night—and I really didn't expect how much it would hurt to see his hands all over you."

Katrina nodded. "I had to allow it…to do it. It became apparent that if I didn't give him what he wanted—his conquest—then I ran the risk of earning his animosity."

"You're very calculating," Juasa said, her expression revealing none of her thoughts. "I hadn't realized how much 'til last night. It kept me up, and got me thinking."

"Oh?" Katrina asked as she walked closer and leaned on one of the crates. "About what?"

"For starters, your 'pinnace', as you call it."

Katrina braced herself, this was the weakest part of her plan. She had hoped to fully win Juasa over before the crew chief put two and two together.

"What about my pinnace?"

"It's brand new. Well, sort of. The tests I ran showed that the hull is only a few decades old…give or take a bit, depending on what it's been exposed to. But it's easy to tell from the drives that your flight into Tsarina was the skiff's maiden voyage. I mean…you could have replaced them, but I've been inside that skiff, it's pristine."

Katrina shrugged. "I've never had the need to use it before."

"And what about the previous owners? Your ship, the *Voyager,* it's an old model. Centuries. There's no way that craft sat unused for that long—and it's another thing that doesn't match."

"What are you suggesting?" Katrina asked, her tone measured, revealing nothing.

"I assume you've secured this room somehow," Juasa said, glancing over Katrina's shoulder at the closed door. "You wouldn't be talking aloud if you hadn't."

Katrina nodded. "We should be in private right now, yes."

"Then I'll lay it out, plain and simple; you're a Streamer," Juasa said, her eyes narrow and her tone accusing. "I don't know why it took me so long to guess. I suppose it's how well you blended in at the bar. If I hadn't known better, I could almost have taken you for a local."

Katrina looked long into Juasa's unblinking eyes and knew there would be no way to dissuade the woman from her conviction. Especially since she was right.

Now it was time to turn her back into an ally.

"You're right, I am," Katrina replied, losing the haughty tone she had affected since arriving at Tsarina. "I came out of the Streamer a few days ago."

Juasa's eyes grew wide. "I knew it!" she whispered loudly, spreading her arms wide. "I knew there was no away a pinnace like yours would never have had a-grav. But why did you lie about—never mind, stupid question."

Katrina took another step toward Juasa, who in turn took one back, bumping into a crate and stopping.

"I don't want to cause you any harm, Juasa. My only goal was to upgrade my ship with FTL and get the hell out of here."

Juasa's eyes narrowed. "Was?"

Katrina looked down at her hands, sheathed in blue, gleaming and flashing. She folded them and clenched her fingers. "Well," she said, looking back up at Juasa as she spoke. "I *still* do want FTL—and to get out of Bollam's. This really isn't my kind of place."

"So what's changed?" Juasa asked.

"In a word? You."

Juasa's face softened and she took a step forward. "You can't be serious, Verisa, we only just met."

Though Juasa's words dismissed the notion of Katrina wanting to be with her, the woman's eyes said something else entirely.

"I feel the same way you do," Katrina said. She took another step toward Juasa and extended her hand. "Is it rational? No. You work for a company that will seize my ship and sell me as a slave—or maybe worse—if they learn I'm a Streamer."

"I know! What were you thinking?" Juasa said as she took Katrina's hand. "My teams are going to figure it out! When the Captain..."

Juasa's eyes widened and she stepped back once more, pulling her hand from Katrina's

"You knew all along. You didn't need my suggestion to seduce and control him, it was your plan from the start. If you were so calculating with him, what part of your scheme do I fit into?"

"None whatsoever—well sorta."

Juasa's lips tightened into a thin line. "Sorta?"

Katrina sighed. "I knew I'd have to sway the workers in some fashion. I figured I'd go through the captain for that. I didn't plan on meeting you—you sought me out, remember?"

"For a ride!" Juasa retorted. "Took a good bit to work up the courage to approach you, too. All aloof in your expensive clothes."

"This isn't me," Katrina said and gestured at her body, perfectly outlined in the azure skinsheath. "This is someone who will impress KiStar and Captain Ferris. My only plan was to seduce him, and then offer him a stasis pod to keep his mouth shut. It would be enough to get him a leg up."

"You're going to have to offer a lot more than that. You may get Ferris on your side, but I don't think you have enough time to get Anna between the sheets as well."

Katrina nodded. "Anna wouldn't require that treatment. I could get her with the pods, no sexual favors required."

"Is that what you do?" Juasa asked sharply. "Just fuck whoever you need to get whatever you want?"

"Oh, you have no idea..." Katrina's voice drifted off. "I used to, a long, long time ago. I was a spy for my government, but I changed sides when I met a man that captured both my heart and my mind. He was the strongest, bravest man I ever met. I spent a century with him."

"Why did you leave him?" Juasa asked, her tone sharp, but her expression immediately apologetic for sounding so harsh.

Katrina could tell that Juasa was wavering. She still didn't trust the story being related, but she wanted to. Lucky for Katrina, the truth was all Juasa would need to hear to understand—she hoped. Then she could stop lying to this woman who strangely meant so much to her.

"I didn't," Katrina said. "He left me—died of old age, the stubborn old fool."

"Really?" Juasa asked. "He must have been robbing the cradle. You don't look old at all, I mean, there are some wrinkles in the corners of your eyes, but those look sex—" Juasa stopped herself before continuing. "How old was he when he died?"

Katrina laughed and ignored the question. "Sexy, you say? Thank you. I was trying not make too drastic a change during my last rejuv."

"Yeah, well, I liked the older aristocratic thing you had going on. Now I wonder how affected it was."

"Maybe I should start from the beginning."

"I think that would be a great thing to do."

Katrina took a deep breath. "I was born with the name Katrina in 4122, on Incandus, capital world of the Sirius System. I grew up in the house of a government CEO, and eventually joined the Luminescent Society's spy organization that kept an eye on the Noctilucent workers around Sirius."

"Fucking stars in the black, you're an *ancient*," Juasa whispered.

Katrina laughed. "Not quite that old; I'm not yet two-hundred in biological years."

Juasa shook her head and looked around the bay, her expression growing worried. "I mean you're from the time of the ancients, at the height of civilization, the golden age of humanity," Juasa's voice dropped to a whisper as she spoke.

"If anyone learns of this, you're screwed. We're both screwed!"

Katrina reached out and put a hand on Juasa's arm. "Remember, I have the room secured. Our activities and conversations in here are being faked and fed into the ship's monitoring logs. We're safe."

Juasa nodded, and a look of curiosity came over her. "So, Ver— uh, Katrina, how did you end up in the Streamer?"

"I hit it not long after leaving Kapteyn's Star," Katrina replied. "I was searching for some friends, who I now believe also fell prey to the Streamer."

"Kapteyn's…" Juasa said and tilted her head, looking off as she accessed the Link. "Katrina, if you were at Kapteyn's… noooooooo."

Juasa's eyes met Katrina's, wide with amazement.

"Holy shit, you don't look quite like her, but there was a Katrina who was governor of Kapteyn's; the wife of the first leader, Markus."

"That was me," Katrina replied.

"You…you were the president of a star system? What are you doing here? Are you alone?"

"Yes, I was the president for a time, and I'm here searching for some friends, remember? Lastly, yes, I came alone, well, sort of."

"Sort of?"

"There's an AI with me—on the *Voyager*."

Juasa whistled. "This is a lot to take in— Wait. You knew that I would figure this out, didn't you?"

Katrina nodded. "I did. I mean, anyone would have the moment they realized that I didn't have *broken* a-grav systems. I have *no* a-grav systems."

Juasa's hands perched on her hips and her brow lowered. "So if you were going to trade pods for the repairs, and buy off the captain with pods, what did you think my price would be?"

"After I met you, after what we got up to on my pinnace…I was hoping maybe nothing."

"Nothing?" Juasa asked, her tone growing acidic. "Am I that much of a cheap date? One round—albeit a really good one—between the sheets, and I'm bought and paid for?"

Katrina shook her head, and reached for Juasa's hand once more, clasping it between hers. Juasa's expression didn't soften, but she didn't pull her hand back, either.

"No, Juasa, I was going to ask you to come with me."

The words hung between them. This was it, the moment where Katrina gained an ally or made an enemy—or at least someone else that she had to buy off.

Juasa's eyes narrowed. "How do I know that you're not just playing me? You seem to be an adept."

Katrina lowered her eyes. "Juasa, I have hundreds of stasis pods. I have other tech that would make you a queen here—from what I can see of modern tech, at least. Do you want it? It's yours."

She looked up and met Juasa's eyes. She could see that the woman was considering what life could be like with whatever ungodly amounts of credit such technology would earn her.

Katrina hoped Juasa wouldn't take that offer.

"Until a day ago," Katrina continued, "I had one goal in life: to find my friends. But yesterday…after so long since Markus…. Let's just say that I wouldn't mind adding you to my list of things to live for. Stars, that's so corny—if you think that I'm saying this to win you over with my spycraft, you're wrong. There are a hundred better options than to make an impassioned plea for you to run away with me."

Juasa stretched out her other hand and wrapped it around Katrina's. "I don't think it's corny at all. Though I'll admit that

I, too, feel silly for falling head over heels for someone so quickly. What does that make the two of us?"

Katrina laughed as she stepped in and lowered her lips to Juasa's. "I think it makes us lucky."

Juasa's arms encircled Katrina and slid down her back, while Katrina reached up and pulled the smaller woman into her, sliding her fingers into Juasa's hair, gripping it tightly.

"Oh, stars, how do you do this to me?" Juasa asked as she pulled her lips far enough from Katrina's to speak. "I want to kiss you *everywhere* right now, but we can't. Eventually someone will come in here—plus we'll have to leave and not look like we...."

"You're right," Katrina said and pulled her hand from Juasa's hair, smoothing it carefully. She did not, however, remove her other arm, nor did Juasa unwrap hers.

"Am I enough? Enough of a trade?"

Juasa snorted. "Do you have any idea how much I hate this star system? You could have told me back at the bar that you wanted a fuck buddy for long interstellar flights, and I would have bailed on KiStar in a heartbeat—not that that's all I want out of this."

"Me either," Katrina replied. "I was fully prepared to spend the rest of my life without taking another lover...just to search for my friends and settle down with them."

"Wait..." Juasa looked into Katrina's eyes, though they were unfocused as she searched over the Link. "These friends... they're not.... No! They must be! You're looking for the *Intrepid*!"

"You know about it?" Katrina asked, her voice rising in pitch. "Has anyone seen it?"

Juasa shook her head, her lips parted with wonder. "You were governor when the *Intrepid* was at Kapteyn's, it's in the history records—you set foot on that ship. You saw their picotech!"

"That cat's out of the bag then, is it?" Katrina asked. "Was probably too much to hope that the picotech would stay a secret forever."

Juasa drew her hands up Katrina's back and rested them on her shoulders. "Katrina. The *Intrepid* is the most sought after prize of any system along the Streamer. Everyone knows that if they find the *Intrepid,* they'll be set for life."

"Ha! They think that they could just seize the *Intrepid*?" Katrina asked with a laugh. "Now that is something I'd like to see."

Juasa frowned. "Why's that? I thought they were your friends."

"Oh, they are," Katrina answered with a chuckle. "I just pity whoever tries to take that ship. Tanis will not go down without a fight."

"Tanis…"

"She's the XO on the *Intrepid,* and the commander of its fleets. More importantly, she's the one with the guts to use picotech when she must."

"Then it *is* real," Juasa breathed. "The ship really does have picotech. Do you?"

Katrina shook her head. "No, and I'm glad I don't. I don't want to have that kind of power."

Neither woman spoke for a minute and then Juasa laughed. "I can't believe this. I meet an ancient at some bar and beg a ride from her. Turns out that she's from the place and time with the most coveted technology in the galaxy, and she's on a quest to find the ship that possesses it. It's like I'm in some sort of fantasy story."

"Well, it'll be a horror story if we don't figure out how to get the *Voyager* upgraded and get the heck out of here," Katrina replied. "I hope you have an idea about how we can upgrade the ship without tipping off that it's a Streamer vessel."

"I have a plan," Juasa replied. "But it's going to take Carl's help."

*****

Carl looked at the pair of women, raised an eyebrow in disbelief, and then began to laugh.

Katrina looked at Juasa and the crew chief sighed.

"Carl, it's not a joke. Look at Katrina. Does she seem like the sort of person who flies around space pranking people?"

Carl's laughter only increased and before long he was gasping for breath—trying to speak, but failing miserably.

"I think we'll have to let him get it out of his system," Katrina said.

Eventually Carl's laughter died down, and he straightened up and placed his hands on his hips, looking back and forth between Juasa and Katrina.

"OK…I just want to make sure I get this straight," he began, and another laugh escaped his throat before he quelled it. "You, Verisa; your name is actually Katrina, and you're an ancient in search of the *Intrepid*. Your ship doesn't have FTL, so your plan was to get a repair ship out into the black to install grav emitters, and hope you could somehow swindle everyone not to just take your ship and sell you off?"

Katrina nodded. "In a nutshell, yes. But I would prefer the both of you to call me Verisa. We can't have any slip-ups."

"And what makes you think I'll go along with this?" Carl asked.

Juasa walked across the maintenance bay and stood before Carl, her hands clasped. "Because you're a good man, Carl. We've known each other forever, and I need your help. Please."

"Yeah, good man," Carl said as he reached up and pulled at his collar. "See where that's gotten me? Did you know that my piece of shit brother paid off his debt and is now free again? Did he put one goddamn red cent toward the part *I* took over? Nope! I still owe a decade's worth of wages to pay for that…that fucker's freedom."

"Shit, Carl, I didn't know," Juasa said, her tone genuinely apologetic.

"Yeah, how would you?" Carl asked. "You've been too busy pining after our high-class guest here while she fucked the captain."

"OK, Carl, that's not fair. A lot has been going on, and I'm really sorry that your brother screwed you over, but maybe we can figure something out. Katrina has a lot of tech. Certainly enough to pay off your debts."

Carl looked at Juasa, and then over her shoulder at Katrina. "What did you offer her for her help?"

Katrina smiled. "Nothing."

Carl's eyes darted back to Juasa. "Nothing? Really?"

Juasa chuckled. "Well, not nothing. Katrina's taking me with her."

Carl reached up and stroked his chin, walking away from Juasa, and then back again. "So your ship. It's as big as you've said?"

"Yes," Katrina replied, guessing at where this was going. "It was built as an evac ship for a research facility. It can hold four hundred people, in a pinch."

Carl's eyes met Juasa's and he shook his head. "She could take us all."

Juasa nodded. "I'd thought of that, but I don't know if everyone would want to come. What about Rory and Mal?"

"We could cut them out," Carl said. "But the rest, the rest would kill to get out of Bollam's."

Juasa looked back at Katrina. "So, how do you feel about having a crew?"

Katrina honestly had no idea. Until a minute before, she had only thought of how delightful it would be to continue her search for the *Intrepid* with Juasa at her side.

But a crew…a good crew is like a family. So long as we share the same goals.

"I can't say I can offer permanent positions or anything, but if we get FTL on the *Voyager*, I'd be more than happy to take anyone wherever they want to go."

Carl nodded. "That's a good enough start. Now we just have to get the captain to think all this is his idea."

Katrina gave a sad laugh. "I think that particular task falls to me."

SACRIFICE

STELLAR DATE: 11.15.8511 (Adjusted Gregorian)
LOCATION: KSS *Havermere,* en route to *Voyager*
REGION: Scattered Disk, Bollam's World System (58 Eridani)

Katrina moaned with feigned delight and clawed gently at Ferris's chest as he finished. He gazed down at her with a possessive look before pulling back and collapsing on the bed next to her.

She bit back an unhappy sigh—as well as the half dozen things she wanted to say—and instead spoke softly in a breathy voice. "Strong captain *and* amazing lover…you're wasted out here on this repair boat."

It wasn't a complete lie. Ferris was moderately competent in bed, but certainly not a patch on Juasa. If he could figure out how to keep his pride out of his quest for her affections, he might have learned what she had to offer.

Ferris chuckled. "You've noticed, have you? It's not all bad, though. The *Havermere* is a good ship, and I have a good crew, mostly. But I've always wanted more. There's a ceiling at a place like KiStar; there aren't any ships bigger or better than this one in the KSS fleet, and once Uriah proves out through her stint as the company sales flack, she'll get the reins."

"It's certainly a strange way to handle succession," Katrina said.

"Yeah," Ferris said, sliding his hands behind his head.

Katrina could tell what he was thinking about, and it wasn't her. The captain was probably wondering what it would be like to have Uriah next to him.

"I might be able to help you on a road to something better," Katrina said quietly. "I have some means at my disposal."

Ferris turned on his side to face her, an eyebrow raised. "Oh yeah, what sort of means?"

"Do you remember the tech I'm taking to Sol?"

"Mmhhhhmmm," Ferris responded. "There's more than one betting pool running on the *Havermere* as to what it may be."

"In a word, stasis," Katrina replied.

Ferris half sat up, propping himself on his elbow. "What? Like pods?"

Katrina nodded. "Yeah, pods."

Ferris whistled, falling onto his back. "I don't even know what a stasis pod would go for."

"Here? Yeah, I can't even imagine," Katrina replied. "I bet you could retire on it, though."

"Yeah," Ferris said with a snort. "But the White Queen and her father at KiStar wouldn't take too kindly to me getting in on action like that, though."

"What if I paid for the upgrades with stasis pods? Let them in on the deal?" Katrina asked. "My buyer in Sol doesn't know exactly how many I have—I didn't want to commit to him before I secured the cargo. But you've been such a generous host, and I know your crews are going to do great work. It seems like it would be a shame not to help you out as much as I'm able."

Ferris rubbed his chin. "Jan could probably work out a price; I'm sure that it wouldn't take many pods to pay for it—they're probably each worth as much as the *Havermere*."

Katrina traced a hand across Ferris's chest, and then brought a finger to his chin. "In that case, how do you feel about two?"

"I could buy an interstellar freighter and stock it with whatever I wanted with that kind of credit..." he locked eyes with Katrina. "And you? What do you get out of this? That's quite the haul for someone flying an older model with bad grav emitters."

Katrina chuckled. "Well, I haven't sold them *yet*. I got them in a bit of a…windfall."

"Oh, yeah?" Ferris asked with a grin on his lips. "I knew you were more than just a pretty face. You're a schemer, aren't you?"

Katrina winked at Ferris and traced a finger down his chest. "I've been known to hatch a plan in my day. But what do I get out of you in trade, Captain Ferris? I want your protection. Your crew is going to see my cargo; I don't want them thinking that they can walk off with it—or mutiny against you and take it all for themselves. Anna seems like the sort that might consider a move like that."

Ferris sat up in bed and glanced down at Katrina before nodding to himself. "She might be, yeah. She always has been grasping."

"Then what's your plan?"

"Well, for starters, we will need to talk to Jan. Nothing happens without her giving a price on the pods. If it's solid, then we work out a deal."

"And how are we going to do the work?" Katrina asked. "I don't trust Juasa; she's been shifty ever since I arrived."

"Yeah," Ferris nodded. "She has issues. But I can sideline her and put Carl in charge of the repairs. I can buy him off easily enough. His brother has some serious debts—it's why Carl is indentured. He had to take on part of the load. He'll do what he's told."

"And he has a select few discrete workers?" Katrina asked.

"Yeah, I'm certain of it," Ferris replied.

"Well, then," Katrina said as she pulled Ferris back down toward her. "I think we should seal this deal with a kiss."

Ferris laughed as he reached around and slapped her ass. "I think a little bit more than a kiss is warranted."

REPRIEVE

STELLAR DATE: 11.16.8511 (Adjusted Gregorian)
LOCATION: KSS *Havermere,* en route to *Voyager*
REGION: Scattered Disk, Bollam's World System (58 Eridani)

Katrina felt like an errant schoolgirl, sneaking off to have a tryst with her lover as she waited in her pinnace for Juasa to arrive.

Except she had never done anything like sneak off and have trysts as a schoolgirl. She had lived under her father's iron rule, with barely a spare moment.

Perhaps this whole wild chase after the *Intrepid*—culminating in her affair with Juasa—was her mid-life crisis.

A soft click reached her ears, and Juasa appeared in the back of the cabin, entering through the maintenance hatch that was currently open in the belly of the ship.

"Katrina," Juasa whispered as she approached with a tender smile on her lips.

"Verisa," Katrina cautioned. "We can't have slip-ups. How did the team take it?"

"Take it?" Juasa asked with a laugh. "They're exuberant. Thank stars that we reach your ship tomorrow. Keeping them quiet for more than a day may have been impossible."

Katrina tensed. "Do we need to worry?"

Juasa patted her on the shoulder. "Sorry, I was exaggerating. They'll do anything for a ticket out of Bollam's world. Trust me, they won't breathe a word of this."

"Good," Katrina replied. "I have the captain in place, and he's prepared to deal with Anna."

"What about our AI, Sam?" Juasa asked.

"I've altered a lot of the ship's sensors to show what we want. Sam shouldn't pick up anything unusual from the

Voyager. And if he causes problems, I have taps in place that will get my AI, Troy, in so that he can take care of things."

"He'll do that?" Juasa asked. "Go against another AI?"

Katrina nodded. "He will. Troy is very dedicated. He wants to find the *Intrepid* as much as I do."

Juasa looked up into Katrina's eyes. "Really? That seems like a strange thing for an AI to want."

"That's because you've never met Bob," Katrina replied.

"Who's Bob?"

Katrina ran her hands down Juasa's sides. "I have to save some stories for our journey. Right now, I'd rather just get to know you a bit more."

"Oh yeah? Get to know me up here?" Juasa gave a soft laugh and touched her forehead. Then she drew her finger down her body and let it come to a stop between her legs. "Or get to know me here?"

Katrina slid a hand behind Juasa's back and lowered her face to her lover's. "Let's start down there, and maybe I'll work my way up."

Later, as they lay on the bunk, limbs still entwined, basking in the afterglow, Katrina wondered how long this feeling would last.

She thought back to how it had been with Markus—still feeling guilty as she did so, but less now than before. Their early days had been chaotic: getting the *Hyperion* safely out of Sirius, and then dealing with the myriad crises that had cropped up on the journey between the stars.

They never really had a time in their romance that was filled with wild, animalistic passion. Markus had been ever attentive, ever loving, but never primal.

Juasa was almost exclusively primal.

"What are you thinking about?" Juasa asked.

"You," Katrina replied.

"Good answer," Juasa said with a soft laugh. "Seriously, though."

"I am being serious," Katrina said, turning to gaze into Juasa's hazel eyes. "I was thinking about how different this is from the last time I fell in lo—"

She realized what she was saying and stopped herself as Juasa's eyes grew wide.

"You were saying…" Juasa whispered.

Katrina swallowed. Did she really feel that way? What if Juasa didn't? *Nonsense,* she told herself. *The woman has signed up to traipse across the stars with you. She must have real feelings, too.*

"Love." Katrina said at last. "I was thinking about how I've fallen in love with you."

Juasa's eyes were still just as wide, and now her lips had parted. Katrina could see that her heartrate and blood pressure had risen. She hoped the reaction bode well.

"Isn't it a bit soon?" Juasa asked. "Aren't you afraid you're going to jinx it?"

"Juasa," Katrina said as she reached out and smoothed the woman's dark hair. "I'm over two-hundred years old. If I want to be in love with you, I'm going to be in love with you. I don't need to spend months or years to figure it out. I already know it. You don't have to be in love with me, if you're not yet ready. But now you know where I stand."

Juasa gave her light, bubbling laugh. "Verisa's pretty damn hot, don't get me wrong; but now that I'm getting to know the real you? Yeah, I think it's safe to say that I'm in love—just don't get rid of the she-devil skinsheath."

"Deal," Katrina said with a seductive smile as her hand drifted down across Juasa's breasts. "Think you have time to show some proof before you have to go back to your duties?"

Juasa grinned wickedly. "Yeah, I think I have time to lay a bit of my proof on you."

*****

A crew was working in the bay when Juasa and Katrina finished, and, since there was no reason for Katrina not to be on her own ship, she left first.

Juasa heard one of the workers in the bay—Terrance, unless she missed her guess—ask Katrina, or Verisa, rather, what she was up to.

True to form, Verisa shot the man down with a cutting insult, and told him that he should keep his moronic questions to himself.

Then the cockpit's canopy closed, and no further sound came from the bay. Juasa snapped her fingers and chuckled. She would have loved to hear Terrance's response.

Juasa leaned back on the cabin's bunk and pulled up the work schedules. Provided everyone got their shit done on time, no one should be in the bay in thirty minutes, and it would be safe for Juasa to exit through the maintenance hatch in the underside of the pinnace.

She decided it was the perfect time to take a short nap—all the shenanigans with Katrina was starting to take its toll. A bit of sleep would help keep her going till the end of the shift.

Juasa drifted off thinking about what it would be like: flying through interstellar space with Katrina, exploring worlds and cultures, seeing things she had only imagined. It would be a dream come true; one she couldn't wait to embark on.

It didn't feel like any time had passed when Juasa woke with a start. She checked the time over the Link and saw that she had been asleep for over an hour.

"Shit," she swore aloud. She'd missed a meeting with Carl. Hopefully he'd let it slide—though she was certain he'd needle her about it for at least a day.

She began to ease off the bunk when a soft tapping sound echoed through the interior of the pinnace. Juasa froze and listened intently. The sound repeated. It was coming from the canopy. Almost like someone was trying to enter codes into the access panel.

Juasa grabbed her uniform and slowly slipped it on, wishing that the White Queen had picked a color combination that wasn't always the brightest thing on the ship. It made it impossible to sneak around.

A quick look at the hatch in the back of the cabin told her that it *shouldn't* be visible to whoever was trying to get into the pinnace, but if that person tried to peer inside, they might spot her.

She decided that quick and swift was her best bet; crouched low, she scuttled across the deck and slipped through the hatch, which she closed behind her.

Below the cabin's hatch was a small crawlspace between the deck and the hull, and Juasa slithered through it, now thanking Uriah for such smooth and frictionless uniforms.

Ahead was the exterior hatch, and Juasa slowed as she approached, taking care not to make any sounds of her own, while listening for any outside.

None reached her ears, and she slowly slipped out of the hatch, landing hands-first on one of the cradle beams and then slowly lowering down onto her back before rolling forward and rising into a crouch.

She peered around the cradle struts that reached up to support the pinnace and saw no movement. Juasa was just about to move out from under the ship when she heard the sound of someone walking down the ramp.

Sure enough, a pair of legs in a white KiStar uniform came into view, and started walking around the pinnace. Juasa could tell that, whoever it was, they were headed for the lower access trench, and would spot her in a matter of moments.

She reached up and twisted her hair into a messy bun, and then walked out from under the pinnace. "Who's up there messing around?" Juasa asked loudly.

"Ju?" the voice asked, its tone cold.

Juasa muttered a curse as she stepped out to see Anna standing above her on the deck.

"Yeah, who else do you think I am?" Juasa asked. "What are you doing here?"

Anna grinned and shrugged. "Just taking a look into the golden girl's skiff. What are you doing?"

"Working on the stupid thing," Juasa said with a dour look. "She complained to Ferris that there was a secondary system failure on her soap dispenser or some other bullshit and I'm down here working on it."

"Really? The soap dispenser?" Anna asked.

Juasa laughed. "No, but it was funny, right? I'm a regular comedian." *I'm an idiot.* "Problem's in the port chem booster. Just a burned out injector. It's a nonstandard size, so I have to fab an adapter."

"Huh, sounds like fun," Anna said disinterestedly.

"Right," Juasa shot back. "Wanna help? I'm going to be at it for another few hours at least."

"Ha!" Anna barked a laugh. "I'm no grease monkey. Have fun."

The first mate turned and walked away, not turning as Juasa shouted at her back. "That's *Chief* Grease Monkey to you."

When Anna left, Juasa walked back under the ship and sagged against a beam.

<*Katrina?*> she sent the message to the *Havermere*'s subsystem like Katrina had shown her. A moment later, the response came back.

<*Juasa, everything OK?*>

<*Mostly. Caught Anna trying to get into your ship, though.*>

Katrina sent an incredulous look. <*Seriously?*>

<*Yeah, I sent her away using the cover I was working on your ship.*>

<*Good thing you were around,*> Katrina said. <*We haven't been too careful with our DNA in there.*>

Juasa laughed. <*You can say that again. I'm going to give it a full clean. Can you complain to Ferris that something is wrong with your port side engine, like a mixture alert? I told Anna I'm replacing an injector, and that Ferris told me to.*>

<*Shoot, Juasa, that's gonna be a pain in the ass. You'll have to fab a part,*> Katrina replied apologetically.

<*Yeah…I know. Gotta make it look good, though.*>

<*OK, I'll be with him in a moment…he's never far, it seems.*>

Juasa felt a twinge of jealousy, but pushed it down.

<*Yeah, I know what you mean. I'll talk to you later, gotta get to work.*>

<*Sorry again, love,*> Katrina said. <*I'll talk to you soon.*>

Juasa sent a pair of kissing lips Katrina's way, and then cut the connection.

'Love'. Katrina is really knee deep in it. Juasa didn't blame her; she was, too. With a bounce in her step and a whistle on her lips, she pulled herself out of the trench and walked to the bay's tool rack.

Time to get to work. It may take the next four or five hours, but it's worth it for the chance to leave this place.

Especially to leave with Katrina.

COMMUNIQUE

STELLAR DATE: 11.17.8511 (Adjusted Gregorian)
LOCATION: KSS *Havermere*, en route to *Voyager*
REGION: Scattered Disk, Bollam's World System (58 Eridani)

Another day, another session with Ferris in his room.

This, however, had been the last. In a few hours, they would be at the *Voyager*.

Once back in her room, Katrina washed off the stench of Ferris—as much as the sonic shower could. When that was done, she stretched for several minutes, working out kinks in her muscles, and relaxing her body while clearing her mind.

It was a routine that she had picked up during her time as a spy and had kept up with in the intervening years. Always wearing a mask, always pretending at attitudes, reactions, and opinions—it was exhausting work.

Without the routine of grounding herself, Katrina knew that she would start to lose her identity in the personas she created. She would forget who she was and become one of her creations—or something worse: a chameleon who had no real face.

After several minutes, she began her mantra.

"I am Katrina," she whispered. "Daughter of the despot Yusuf, friend of the Noctus, liberator of the *Hyperion*, wife of Markus, president of Victoria, searcher in the dark."

She breathed out, closed her eyes, and breathed back in once more. "I am all of those things, together they are me. They form my foundation, they give me purpose, my memories are my strength, the proof of my convictions."

She bowed her head, touching her chin to her sternum and continued her recitation.

"I am the soft reed that grows along the shore. One foot in the river, one on land. I bend in the wind, I weather the flood, I persist, I survive. I touch all these things, I live in their worlds, but they are not me, and I am not them. I am Katrina."

As she spoke those last words, Katrina placed her legs together, and stretched her arms overhead, imaging herself as the flexible, unbroken reed. She bent over backwards arching her back more and more until her hands reached her ankles, then the floor.

"And even though my world may so often seem upside down," with that she kicked her right leg out and up, followed by her left, now standing on her hands, "it does not change who I am. I continue to be Katrina. I am always myself; nothing less, nothing more."

She held the pose for a minute, concentrating on her breathing, before flexing her arms and pushing off, flipping into the air and landing on her feet.

In front of her was the row of drawers set into the bulkhead. Each one contained a costume, a disguise. One was less so than the others—the black and red skinsheath she bought first on Tsarina.

She pulled it out and flipped it over in her hands, the supple polymer sliding like it was a living thing. Something about the duality of the outfit, the glowing red, contrasted with the dark, light-sucking black, made it feel more like her.

Or maybe it was that she was wearing it when she met Juasa.

Katrina slipped into the outfit and pulled up the fastener, dimming the sheath's glow once it activated. She considered the a-grav boots.

"Why the hell not," she said to herself.

Once the boots were on, Katrina sat at her desk, idly bouncing her feet up and down against the soft a-grav field. She checked over the additional nano she had deposited near the control systems for the ship's comm array, and saw that they had finished creating the bypass circuit that would allow her to send out a tight-beam message.

The ship's logs would not show any outgoing signal, and with her various hacks in place, the sensors were unlikely to pick up the response.

<*Troy, this is Katrina. You still out there?*>

They were still five light seconds away from the *Voyager*'s location; a gap that they would close in the next hour.

She waited for the response and when it came, breathed a long sigh of relief.

<*Of course I am. Where else would I be?*>

Where else indeed.

<*I'm on my way to you with a repair ship that can outfit the* Voyager *with everything we need for FTL travel. However, there have been…complications.*>

<*I've been sniffing what data I can while I've waited,*> Troy replied after the delay. <*I suspect you mean the likelihood that they'll declare us fair game for being Streamers.*>

Katrina nodded, even though she knew he couldn't see it.

<*Yes, there's that. I've been working on a plan to keep us safe. It's involved a lot of sex, swindling, and deals, but I have the captain of this ship in my pocket, and many of the vessel's systems infiltrated. We're going to swap four pods for the repairs, and then pay off the captain with two. Can you have the automatons disconnect them from the stasis bays and stack them in the cargo hold? Maybe do a dozen; we may have to do some last minute convincing.*>

<*Of course. There are spares in storage, it will be easy,*> Troy replied. <*I assume you've got something in mind to keep the repair crews themselves from taking the* Voyager *and running.*>

<*I do. I have formed a relationship with the crew chief, and have been playing her and the captain against one another—sort of. Either way, she's onboard; and so is her second and his top crew.*>

Troy's response took half a second longer than it should have. <*Interesting choice of words, 'on board'.*>

<*Noticed that, did you?*> Katrina asked.

<*I can load balance mass transfer on a ship that's boosting at over seventy gs while traveling at relativistic speeds. Picking up on your nuances is like arithmetic by comparison.*>

<*You're so humble, Troy,*> Katrina replied with a laugh.

<*You have no idea. How many stray pups we taking on?*>

<*Six. The crew chief, Juasa; her second, Carl; and his team. Excepting Juasa, they're all indentured. A ride out of Bollam's World to just about anywhere is a deal they're willing to take.*>

<*And the chief?*> Troy asked. <*What was her price, if not freedom from servitude?*>

<*Just me,*> Katrina replied after a moment.

<*Hold on. Are you telling me that she's coming along because she feels a chemical attraction to you? Are you sure that's wise? I've seen the sims. That always ends badly.*>

Katrina laughed. <*The chemical attraction is mutual. She knows what she's getting into.*>

<*Wait. You told her? How much?*>

<*Everything,*> Katrina replied.

<*Katrina. You're such an…organic. I can't believe you did that.*>

She knew that Troy meant that to be an insult, but she didn't take it as one. <*She was figuring it out, and I'm not as good at hiding who I am as I once was. I didn't want to lie to her anymore.*>

<*Fine. So how do you think this will play out?*>

<*Honestly? I think that we'll at least get the a-grav systems installed before things go sideways.*>

Troy chuckled in her mind. <*Well, at least your little love affair hasn't clouded your judgement too much. You can tell that this is going to fall apart before the end.*>

<*It's not a love affair.*>

<*OK, Katrina.*>

Katrina shook her head. If ever there was an 'OK' that directly translated into 'you keep telling yourself that', it was the one Troy had just uttered.

<*Juasa isn't our problem, and I don't think the repair crew will be, either. What I'm worried about is that either the captain or one of his crew will double-cross us.*>

<*Do they have an AI?*> Troy asked.

<*Yeah, though you'd barely call it such—though it's at least grumpy like you.*>

<*That's something, I suppose. I might be able to get it on our side, if push comes to shove.*>

<*I've also secured some data on local FTL routes,*> Katrina said. <*Passing it along.*>

<*Excellent. I've pulled an update from the local beacon, and have been watching other ships jump in and out. The location I'm waiting in is jump-capable.*>

<*Sounds like you're prepared.*>

Troy's reply was resolute. <*Always.*>

<*I'll see you in a few hours, Troy. Keep your fingers crossed.*>

<*Funny.*>

Katrina passed a command to the nano in the comm systems to disable the connection and resume their previous state. Even if someone had noticed the comm array sending a signal, a diagnostics run wouldn't show anything unusual. A physical inspection of the comm systems' components would be required to uncover what she had done.

She tunneled through one of her other secure connections into the ship's network and reached out to Juasa.

<*Are you ready?*>

<*As I'll ever be. I can't believe we're doing this,*> Juasa replied.

<*It's going to go off without a hitch,*> Katrina lied. A perfect execution would be a miracle. <*Ready for Ferris to earn his asshole badge?*>

<*Trust me, he has a mountain of those already.*>

They spoke further, reviewing the plan's details, but eventually Juasa begged off to attend to some of her team.

Katrina signed off from the desk and removed all traces of the hacks she had performed from its interface. Now that she had compromised the *Havermere*'s network, she could perform future hacks from nearly any point on the ship—even wirelessly, if she chose, though that had a greater risk of detection.

Once the cleanup was done, Katrina pulled her case out of the cupboard where she had stowed it, and activated its a-grav system, smiling with delight as it floated up before her.

She quickly packed her outfits, gave the room one last visual and nano sweep, and then walked to the door. She paused for it to open, and then strode out into the corridor.

It was time to return to the *Voyager*.

VOYAGER

STELLAR DATE: 11.17.8511 (Adjusted Gregorian)
LOCATION: KSS *Havermere,* approaching the *Voyager*
REGION: Scattered Disk, Bollam's World System (58 Eridani)

Ferris and Anna were waiting for her outside her room.

"My lady!" Ferris exclaimed. "You look incredible!"

"Thank you," Katrina replied, while inclining her head graciously. She noted that even Anna's normal narrow gaze had given way to a wide-eyed look. "However, I don't think I need an escort. I know the way back to the docking bay."

"Of course you do," Ferris said. "I just thought it fitting that I escort you off, as I escorted you aboard."

He offered his arm and Katrina slipped hers around it. They began to walk down the hall, and Anna stayed abreast on Katrina's right side.

The situation made her skin crawl. Ferris walking her down was expected. But Anna? That was not something she had anticipated.

"I understand that Carl has put together an estimate of four days to install the new graviton emitters," Katrina said.

That wasn't entirely true. Carl and Juasa were certain they could install the emitters in two days. The work wouldn't be pretty, but it would get them dumped into the dark layer and on their way somewhere that wasn't Bollams's World.

The installation could be finessed at a later date.

"That is the estimate that Carl has provided me as well," Ferris replied. "The test runs will take a few days longer, of course, but I have no reason to believe it will take him longer than that."

"And Juasa?" Katrina asked. "How has she taken her demotion?"

Ferris chuckled. "Better than I expected. Normally she'd scream at me for an hour over something like this, but this time she only went on for twenty minutes or so."

Anna snorted. "So you're wearing her down, then?"

"Yup," Ferris grinned. "From here on out, she'll be happy for whatever scraps I give her."

"I never asked; how is it that you can pull her off the job? I thought she didn't report directly to you?" Katrina pressed.

"Oh, I have my ways," Ferris said. "I've been working up a report of all the shit she's gotten up to since she came aboard. If I ever send it in, she'll be fired or collared—maybe both. Either way, I pretty much own her now."

"Just like you've always wanted," Anna said, giving a caustic laugh.

Katrina wondered about the relationship between these two. Anna wasn't as beautiful as Juasa, but she was still a very attractive woman. Yet Ferris seemed to have no desire to bed or control her.

Perhaps Anna had something on him; or maybe she had no interest in men. Katrina had certainly noticed a few looks from her over the last couple days—and minutes.

They reached the lift, and Ferris gestured for the two women to enter first. Once inside, Anna turned to Katrina and gave her a sweet smile. "I know what you're up to, and I want in."

"Up to?" Katrina asked archly.

"I had to bring her in on the stasis pods," Ferris said with a sigh. "Anna's very persistent. Once she saw that it was a goods trade and not credit, she badgered Jan till we had to give in."

Katrina nodded. "I figured you'd wise up, Anna. You don't seem like a slouch. I'm prepared to offer you one stasis pod for your silence."

Anna glanced at Ferris, then back at Katrina. "Why's he get two?"

"Because I have to bribe half the ship with my cut from the sales," Ferris said. "Take your pod and be happy. It's more money than you were ever going to earn in your life, anyway."

Anna looked like she was going to say something in response to Ferris, but then closed her mouth and nodded. "Fine."

When the lift doors opened, Anna didn't leave, and Katrina walked out with Ferris.

"She's a bit pushy," Katrina said once the doors closed and they were alone.

"Yeah, sorry about that. She thinks she's above herself, but she's a decent first mate, so I let her get away with it from time to time."

Katrina held back a comment about how it seemed like Anna had just walked all over him, and instead gave the captain a winning smile. "I understand. She needs to feel valued, so you let her assert herself on occasion."

"Exactly." Ferris nodded. "'You catch more flies with honey', and all that."

They reached the bay, and Katrina walked toward the ramp to her pinnace, with Ferris following her aboard.

Katrina paused and turned around. "Did I miss something?"

Ferris shook his head. "Maybe. I thought that it'd be obvious. I need to come over to inspect the merchandise."

Katrina looked around the bay. "Without Jan?"

"She'll be over in a bit with Carl's crew. I figured since you're going, and I'm going, we may as well go together."

Dammit!

Katrina laughed and nodded with a coy smile. "I know what you want. Well, come on then; get onboard."

Once inside the pinnace, Katrina stowed her case, and then sat in the pilot's seat and pulled on her harness.

"Expecting a bumpy ride?" Ferris asked quizzically.

"This pinnace is a relic," Katrina replied. "No a-grav."

"Huh," Ferris said as he looked around. "Seems new."

Katrina gave a soft laugh as she activated the navigation systems and ran a pre-flight check. "Juasa said the same thing. The *Voyager*'s previous owner was a bit of a collector. He liked things that looked like they were from a bygone era."

"Well, he did a good job restoring it, that's for sure," Ferris said.

"You going to stop fondling my pinnace's cockpit and put on your harness so we can go?"

Ferris snorted. "Pushy!"

"You like me pushy," Katrina said with a smirk.

"Yeah, you can say that again."

Ferris put on his harness without further comment, and Katrina signaled to the bay chief that they were ready for takeoff.

The *Havermere*'s docking bay powered up its launch beam, lifted the pinnace off the cradle, and pushed it out into space.

Once they were beyond *Havermere*, Katrina spun the pinnace with its attitude jets and then gave a short burn on the chem booster to send them toward the *Voyager*.

Her ship was on the far side of the *Havermere*, and Katrina deftly steered the pinnace under the repair ship's hull.

"Not a bad pilot," Ferris said. "I half expected you to use a comp to take you over."

"I've picked up a few useful skills over the years," Katrina said and then let out a long sigh. "Ah…there she is."

The *Voyager* looked just as it had when last Katrina laid eyes on it. Matte grey, almost invisible without its running lights, and long and sleek—but flattened, like a narrow manta ray.

"That sure is a nice ship," Ferris commented. "In really good shape, too."

"I take care of my things," Katrina said, and ran a hand along the cockpit's console for emphasis. "There's too much junk in the galaxy. I like to surround myself with beauty."

"You excel at that," Ferris replied.

Katrina picked up an EM signal from the *Voyager* and Linked with it, glad to finally be connected to an advanced network once more.

<*Coming in, Troy,*>

<*I can see that,*> the AI replied. <*I can also see into your cockpit. Who's the passenger?*>

Katrina passed a long-suffering sigh over the Link. <*My good friend Captain Ferris. He wants to 'inspect the merchandise'.*>

<*Why do I get the feeling you're not referring to the stasis pods?*> Troy replied.

<*Automatons get all of them stacked up?*> Katrina asked.

<*Yes, and I scrubbed as much as I could from the ship and our networks that revealed where we're from.*>

Katrina gave a mental head shake. Troy was always overprepared. <*Good thing, I suspect that Ferris will want to stay for a bit.*>

<*What's your plan for him?*> Troy asked.

<*Kick him out the airlock just as soon as we're ready to go.*>

<*Seems excessive.*>

Katrina sent a mental laugh. <*That's because you haven't met him yet.*>

<*I have just one more question,*> Troy said. <*I received a message from Carl outlining the crew that is coming over to work on the ship. Your friend Juasa is not with them. How will you get her out of Bollam's if she's not aboard?*>

<*Earning the captain's favor involved getting her kicked off this job. Carl has a plan to get her over, though. I'm not worried. Yet.*>

<OK, you're the boss. I'm opening the bay doors for you,> Troy replied.

<Gotcha, be aboard in just a few minutes.>

Katrina guided the pinnace toward the ship's cargo bay. The bay's doors slowly opened as they approached; the interior protected by an ES field that held the ship's atmosphere in.

"Where did you buy this thing?" Ferris asked as he leaned forward, peering through cockpit's window at the *Voyager*. "She's a beaut."

"Collector in the Praesepe Cluster," Katrina replied. "He'd kept her in perfect condition."

"Can say that again," Ferris murmured.

The pinnace slipped through the ES shield, and Katrina brought it toward a cradle on the far side of the bay, making room for the repair crew's shuttle to follow. She spun the ship deftly, and set it down on the cradle—which was on the wall, as compared to their orientation aboard the *Havermere*.

"I saw from your rough specs that this thing has stacked decks, but it's something again to see it in person," Ferris said.

"Yeah, it's odd at first," Katrina replied. "But this girl can put down 25*g*s of thrust. Having to handle that lateral motion with dampeners takes a lot more energy if the decks aren't stacked."

"Probably doesn't feel as weird, either," Ferris replied.

Katrina nodded as she undid her harness, and then opened the cockpit's canopy.

The *Havermere*'s supply shuttle was coming into the bay as Katrina carefully swung around and hooked her feet into straps on the bay's floor.

"Shit, I'm out of practice in zero-*g*," Ferris said as he drifted above her. "A hand?"

Katrina laughed and reached up, grabbing Ferris's foot and pulling him down so that he could hook a boot in a floor strap.

"Those them?" he asked, gesturing to twelve crates stacked along one of the bay's walls.

"You bet," Katrina replied. "Stasis pods, lost in some vault on the far side of nowhere."

"Now somewhere," Ferris said wistfully

They waited for the *Havermere*'s shuttle to land and Carl's crew to exit. Though the workers were all wearing EVA suits, they had their helmets off.

The suits possessed maglock boots, and they all clanked across the bay toward the pair; all save Jan, who was only wearing her standard KiStar uniform, and floated awkwardly behind the work crew.

"With your permission, we'll begin our assessment," Carl said. "Mandy and Rama will stay here and guide the components in."

Katrina looked over Carl's shoulder to see a number of cargo pods drift off the top of the *Havermere* and begin to boost toward the *Voyager*.

"Very well," Katrina replied. "Mind Troy, and do as he says," Katrina replied.

"Troy?" Ferris asked as Jan reached them.

Katrina nodded. "Ship's AI. Don't think I'd leave my girl out here alone, did you?"

"No, of course not," Ferris replied.

Katrina led the captain and corporate bean counter to the crates containing the stasis pods. One was conveniently located in front of the stack, and Katrina flipped open the lid, revealing the pod within.

Ferris drew in a sharp breath, while Jan leaned over, her expression intent on the features of the pod.

"Looks Solar," she said.

"Looks like a cryopod," Ferris replied. "But really simple…"

"Cryopods have to freeze things—very quickly, too," Katrina said. "Plus there's all that nasty blood removal they need to manage. Stasis is the cessation of subatomic motion. Just takes the field emitter and a containment vessel."

"I'll need to test it, Jan said."

"Of course," Katrina replied. She reached down and pushed the large button on the pod's side. The cover lifted off and the interior illuminated. "You want to hop in?" Katrina said.

Jan blanched, and Ferris laughed. "She's kidding, Jan, just put your test kit in."

"Yeah, kay," Jan said and pulled a series of devices out of a satchel at her side and set them in the pod.

"How's it powered?" Ferris asked. "I don't see any hookups to the ship."

"Has SC Batts," Katrina replied. "They can keep the stasis field going for years, if needs be. It can also take external power, of course. There's a network beacon on the pod that contains a database of all the features and instructions for maintenance on the pod."

"You've used them, haven't you?" Ferris asked. "The pods, I mean."

"I have," Katrina replied. "In my business, you have to test wares like this. Granted, I didn't test it on myself first."

She smiled as she spoke and let the cracks in her skinsheath widen, filling the corner of the bay with a flickering red light.

Ferris noticed and laughed. "I'm sure you didn't."

"I'm ready," Jan said and stepped back.

Katrina keyed in the commands on the stasis pod, and the cover lowered. Once it did, there was a snap and a hum, and then the interior went dark.

Not just a little bit dark, but completely dark.

"What happened?" Ferris asked.

"It's stasis," Katrina replied. "No atomic motion. No photons, nothing."

"Huh…I guess I never thought of that. How's it work?"

Katrina laughed. "Ferris, you crack me up sometimes, 'how's it work'. If we knew that, we'd all have stasis pods and these things wouldn't be worth the price of a starship."

Ferris smiled, accepting the jibe. "Good point."

They stood for a minute as Jan stared intently at the pod. "OK, that's long enough."

Katrina reached in and disabled the stasis system and the pod slid open. Within, the testing devices appeared exactly as they had. Jan tentatively reached in and retrieved the first one, examining it, and then reached in for the next.

When she had checked them all over, she looked up at Ferris.

"Honestly, I expected this to be a scam…but it's real. These are stasis pods."

Ferris let out a small cry of joy and then wrapped an arm around Katrina's shoulders—almost sending them spinning across the bay, if not for Katrina's foot securely anchored in a foot strap.

"Sweet stars above, this is it! The jackpot," Ferris crowed.

"I assume you need to test the five that we agreed to for the repairs?" Katrina asked Jan.

"Why don't you test a few more," Ferris suggested to Jan. Just in case the work requires anything extra, or Katrina decides that she wants to get some other upgrades performed."

Jan's eyes narrowed, and then she nodded. "Very well, I'll do eight or so."

"Excellent," Ferris said. "Now Katrina, I'd love to see more of this lovely ship of yours."

"Of course, I—" Katrina began, but was interrupted by Jan.

"Umm…how am I supposed to get the rest of the crates unstacked?" she asked.

"Oh, of course," Katrina said. "I did notice that you weren't that adept in zero-*g*."

"No, not so much."

Katrina signaled an automaton, which stepped out of a recess on the side of the bay. "That's Jonnie-5. He'll follow your verbal commands and help you out."

<*Make sure she doesn't accidentally kill herself,*> Katrina requested of Troy.

<*Now where's the fun in that?*>

Katrina sent Troy a dark look as she took Ferris's hand and led him across the bay to the central ladder shaft.

"No lift?" he asked.

"Of course," Katrina lied. "But you don't really want to take a lift in zero-*g*. It's a great way to slam your head into something."

"Good point. I've already proven that I'm no good at no-grav," Ferris chuckled at his own joke. "But I sure can think of something I'd like to try with you."

Katrina pulled Ferris close and put her finger on his lips. "I thought you'd never ask."

INSTALLATION

STELLAR DATE: 11.17.8511 (Adjusted Gregorian)
LOCATION: *Voyager*
REGION: Scattered Disk, Bollam's World System (58 Eridani)

Carl shook his head as he saw Katrina lead Ferris up the ladder, presumably toward her quarters.

"Talk about taking one for the team," he muttered, and Camille laughed.

"I don't care who she screws. She could try and get into the White Queen's ass and I'd applaud her, if it gets us out of Bollam's."

<Please, keep conversations like that to a minimum,> a voice said over the Link. *<Jan is still in the bay, and you never know when ears might be listening.>*

<I hope you appreciate the irony in that statement,> Carl said to Troy. The AI had already introduced himself, and Carl was learning what Katrina had meant when she referred to the artificial intelligence as 'a bit touchy'.

<I do. Now, is this a suitable location?>

Carl examined the room they were in. It was a cabin with a half-meter porthole, and access to the main trunk line for the ship's power.

He grabbed his pad and reviewed the ship and its mass balancing.

<Try this,> Troy said, and suddenly a holographic display appeared in the room. Within it, a semi-transparent image of the ship hovered, their current location highlighted by a yellow marker. *<These purple lines are the balance points for the ship's mass, and these blue lines are the thrust vectors from the main engines. The Orange line is the thrust vector from the AP drive.>*

"Handy," Carl muttered as he hooked his datapad back on his belt. "OK, yeah, this should do. Camille, go help Kirb get the first emitter and the install kit, and get it up here. If Jan asks why we're not doing the teardown first, just tell her we're getting things in place before we pull the old emitters out."

"You got it, boss," Camille said.

<Jan has finished checking the third stasis pod,> Troy said. *<I'd appreciate it if one of you took her back as soon as she's done.>*

Carl considered that Ferris could be 'entertaining' Katrina for some time, and agreed with Troy. Waiting for Ferris could take forever, and the sooner Jan was off the ship, the better.

<Let me know the moment she's done, and we'll fly her and the eight pods back over to the Havermere.*>*

<Five. From what I see, she only knows about the five pods,> Troy said.

<Troy,> Carl said with a laugh. *<If I wasn't able to hide shit from Jan, I would have been locked up years ago. Don't worry, we'll send back all eight pods so that Anna doesn't get suspicious.>*

Troy didn't reply, and Carl assumed the AI must be satisfied.

<I'm going to go check out the bow location. I assume the bridge is just up the ladder?>

<Yes,> Troy said.

Carl pulled himself out of the room and then down the hall. He pushed of a bulkhead out into the ladder shaft and caught a rung.

He gave a deft kick and sailed up the shaft. As he passed deck four, he heard a piercing scream, and then a long moan.

"Taking one for the team," he murmured with a smile.

PHASE 2

STELLAR DATE: 11.17.8511 (Adjusted Gregorian)
LOCATION: KSS *Havermere*
REGION: Scattered Disk, Bollam's World System (58 Eridani)

Juasa watched through a porthole as Katrina's pinnace pulled away from the *Havermere,* and tried to fight back the sinking feeling that she wasn't going to see her again.

A thousand things could go wrong with their plan, and though they had contingencies, a thousand things could go wrong with those too.

Most of those things were in the form of the other officers and crew aboard the *Havermere.*

There were two separate problems to worry about there. The indentured workers—many of whom served under Juasa—and, well...everyone else.

No one would be happy if they found out that Juasa, Carl, and his team of four were going to get out of Bollam's, free and clear—with an ancient and her ship, no less.

Yet Katrina had seemed so confident about the plan, and Juasa had felt that confidence as well. Right up until Katrina left, followed by Carl and his team.

Now she was alone on the *Havermere.*

Stop it, Juasa, she said sternly to herself. *Get a grip and get on with it. You know what needs to be done.*

She turned away from the porthole and the view it provided of the *Voyager*. There was a second shipment of equipment that needed to be stowed on the shuttle once it came back with Jan and the stasis pods. That equipment was going to have a little surprise in it. Namely her.

When Jan returned, she would have the shuttle bring the stasis pods to the *Havermere*'s forward bay, though most of the equipment that needed to go to the *Voyager* was in a rear bay.

It gave Juasa the perfect reason to drive a loader full of crates through the ship, and end up where the shuttle would dock.

When she arrived at Aft Bay #3, the loader was parked near the entrance, and two of her crew were stacking several cases into its bed.

"Hey, Ju," one of the men called, out.

"Howdy, Bill," Juasa replied. "That the last of it?"

"Uhhh..." Bill glanced at his requisitions sheet, and then at the crates in the loader's bed, ticking them off one by one. "Yep, looks like. You want me to drive it up?"

"No, Bill, I got this one. Why don't you and Sal go take the rest of the day off? With us running a small crew on the client ship, there's not much for the rest of us to do."

"Why *are* you running a light crew?" Bill asked.

Juasa gave a rueful laugh. "Bill, Bill, Bill. The captain is over there with his new mistress. If you look out a porthole, you'll see a big sock draped over her ship. He doesn't want much noise, and he wants things to go on as long as possible."

Sal laughed and Bill put a finger alongside his nose. "Ahhh. Gotcha, Chief. Well, if you're giving us the word, then I bet there's a game of Sarel that needs playing."

"Get outta here," Juasa said with a laugh as she swung up into the loader's seat. It didn't really need anyone to drive it to the other bay, but it was KiStar policy that equipment like this couldn't be transported without supervision.

That suited Juasa just fine. Bollam's World had stabilized in recent centuries, clawing its way out of the dark ages. But with that stabilization came more and more advanced NSAI.

If it wasn't for the cheap human labor in the system, she imagined that robots would do most of the jobs out there. Granted, the elites wouldn't get much satisfaction lording over machines. Perhaps humans would have a place for a while, at least.

She signaled the loader over the Link and it lurched into motion, trundling out into the main lateral corridor that ran through the ship.

It was nearly a kilometer to the forward bay, and the trip took just under seven minutes. Normally, Juasa complained—either to herself, or to anyone nearby—about how a small maglev would be a thousand times better.

But this time she enjoyed the ride. Once she reached the forward bay, it would just be a waiting game for Jan to come back with the shuttle.

When the loader arrived at the bay, she directed it to the port-side cradle. As it approached, she saw two of the engineering crew lounging nearby on a pile of seat cushions that had been pulled out of a transit ship that the *Havermere* had serviced the previous month.

"Hey, girls, what's up?" Juasa asked as the loader slowed to a halt.

"Not much," Kelly, one of the two, replied. "Chief Hemry sent us up here to unload and reload the shuttle when it comes back. Said you deserved a break."

Well that puts a crimp in things.

"Did he, now?" Juasa asked. "Isn't that sweet. Don't worry 'bout it, though. I have this covered."

Kelly and her friend, who Juasa finally remembered as Tali, didn't budge. "Got our orders," Kelly said.

"This is a Repair Crew job, here," Juasa said. "Hemry is a good guy, and I appreciate his help, but he works on *this* ship, I work on the ones out there. This is my show."

Kelly frowned. "Well, I can't just go back—he'll wonder why."

Juasa sighed and pinged Hemry over the Link. <*Hey, Hems, how come two of your girls are here insisting that they're going to load my shuttle?*>

<*Oh, you mean Kelly and Tali?*> Hemry asked. Something in his tone bothered Juasa, and she was about to ask what was wrong when the shuttle passed through the grav shield and approached the cradle.

<*Yeah,*> Juasa replied curtly. <*Just tell them to split. I got this.*>

<*Sorry, Juasa. I have orders from Anna, who says she has orders from the captain. Not much I can do about that. Just take their help, OK?*>

Juasa sighed and killed the connection. Hemry wasn't going to budge. He didn't have any special love for the captain, but he had always been chummy with Anna.

That's what it was. She had seen Kelly and Tali with Anna last time they were on Tsarina station. These two were Anna's girls.

What is Anna up to?

The shuttle touched down and a minute later, Jan walked out.

"Stars, it's good to have gravity again. Didn't know how much I missed it!" she exclaimed.

"Didn't you have gravity on the shuttle?" Juasa asked.

Jan shrugged. "Yeah, and now I have it here, too. I have no idea how that woman managed so long in zero-*g*. She seems way too prissy for something like that.

"Takes all kinds," Juasa replied.

She looked inside the shuttle and saw Mandy give her a nervous wave.

<*Easy, Mandy,*> she said privately.

<*Yeah, easy for you to say. We snuck the last three crates on while Jan was in the san heaving up her lunch. But if she looks back in the racks, she's going to wonder why there are more than five pods.*>

"We have it from here, Jan," Juasa said. "We'll put the crates in the secure lockup, and we'll be good to go."

"I don't think so," a voice said from behind Juasa, and she turned to see Anna enter the bay, with Hemry and a few of the engineering crew following after.

"Shit," Juasa whispered. <*Katrina, if you can hear me… we have a problem. Anna's mutinied.*>

"Trying to call your new mistress?" Anna asked. "Don't think I didn't see how you looked at her. Ferris might be too stupid to know when he's being played, but I'm not. You're offline, Juasa. Sam's un-Linked you."

Juasa felt her connection to the shipnet fall away. She tried to reach Katrina through the maintenance subsystem that they had used to chat, but was disconnected mid-send.

"Did they bring all eight?" Anna asked Jan.

"Uh huh," Jan nodded. "I faked an episode in the san so they could load them up, thinking they were so clever."

"Excellent," Anna said with a broad smile. "Now we just have to wait for the *Verisimilitude* to arrive, and we can finish this up."

Verisimilitude, Juasa knew that name…

"Shit," she whispered. "You sold us out. The *Verisimilitude* is a Blackadder ship."

"'Us' is relative," Jan said as she approached Juasa. "When Anna and I compared notes, we realized that Ferris was going to take a big, tasty piece of the pie, and leave us with the scraps. That's a Streamer ship over there, I have no doubt about it. Thing is, we're all pretty sure you already knew that. You had some sort of side deal planned all along. But now *you've* been sold out, and so has the captain; but the rest of us? We've been dealt in."

Juasa couldn't believe what was happening. That Jan and Hemry would side with Anna against the captain—against KiStar. It was insane.

"I have no idea what you're talking about," Juasa pleaded. "Ferris has been acting weird, not me. I've just been trying to fly under the radar while he proved his virility to Verisa."

As Juasa was speaking, she heard a scream and a thud. She turned to see Kelly pulling Mandy out of the shuttle.

"Stop it, what are you all doing?" Mandy shouted as Kelly grabbed her by the hair.

"Getting you off the shuttle," Kelly said before tossing Mandy to the ground. "Now shut it."

"So what's your plan?" Juasa asked. "Sell these eight pods to the highest bidder, and then tell KiStar we were robbed?"

Anna nodded. "Very close. "Though there's some debate as to whether or not we even go back into Bollam's. The *Havermere*'s FTL capable. We'll be richer than gods, and can go wherever we want. Why would we stay here?"

"And what of Verisa and her ship?" Juasa asked. "Just gonna sell them, too?"

Hemry chuckled and Anna replied, "You're on a roll, Ju. You bet we are. I don't know how much you mean to Verisa, but we're going to try to use you for bait, or as a hostage. Whichever. If Verisa really is so sweet on you, maybe she'll trade her life for yours."

"What about Sam?" Juasa asked as she backed further away from Anna. "How could he go against KiStar?"

"I'm not," Sam said aloud. "But Hemry hasn't given me much choice in the matter...."

"You shackled him?" Juasa asked, her eyes wide. She had always thought that Hemry and Sam got along well.

Hemry shrugged. "He wouldn't play along. There are emergency protocols for a rebellious ship's AI. I enacted them."

Juasa stood dumbfounded for a moment, then turned and ran toward the shuttle.

If I can just get inside and hit the emergency door closure—

She had one foot inside the shuttle when her head snapped back, and she stopped short with a shriek. Juasa twisted to see that Kelly had her by the hair.

"Nice try," the big woman laughed before throwing Juasa to the ground. Tali approached and kicked her in the ribs, and she curled up in a fetal position.

"Please…" Juasa moaned. "Just let me go, I don't know anything…."

"Sure, right after this," Kelly said.

Juasa looked up at her attackers just in time to see a boot slam into her face.

Then everything went black.

SEDUCTION

STELLAR DATE: 11.17.8511 (Adjusted Gregorian)
LOCATION: *Voyager*
REGION: Scattered Disk, Bollam's World System (58 Eridani)

"Wine?" Katrina asked, as Ferris lounged on her bed—or, more accurately, above her bed.

"Always," Ferris replied, then laughed at his own joke. "I have to admit, Verisa, I had wondered about your ship. It's very…sterile; not like I expected your vessel to be. But this, this is more like it."

Katrina had worried about that. Given that her entire time on the *Voyager* had been spent in interstellar space, there hadn't been a lot of opportunity to decorate. The only things she had brought aboard—other than clothing—was the one case of mementos.

However, when she entered her cabin, something quite surprising had greeted her.

Troy had used the fab systems aboard the ship to create a lush apartment with draperies on the bulkheads, carpets on the floors, and a large bed in the center of the room. Pictures adorned the walls, and wooden furniture stood around the edges of the space.

At least half of it was holoprojections; though they were so good, even Katrina could barely separate what was real from what was not.

Ferris seemed completely taken in.

"I hadn't had time to decorate too much before I had to go on this trip," Katrina said. "But once it's done, I'm going to deck out every deck."

Ferris laughed softly. "Well done; you're a regular comedian, Verisa."

"I try," Katrina said as she carefully poured the wine into two pouches. "Not the most elegant thing, but they'll do."

He took a sip and smiled before letting the pouch float freely above him.

"Damn, I love that outfit," Ferris said. "You look like a devil. You should get a tail and horns attached. Or modded on…that would be even better."

"You and your fantasies," Katrina said with a shake of her head.

"I have a lot of them," Ferris replied. "Why don't you polish off that wine, and get over here and find out more of them?"

Katrina complied and drank the wine. A little emotional numbing would be nice right about now. She reached up to pull her outfit's fastener out of its hidden groove, but Ferris held up his hand.

"Why don't you leave that on; you're not going to need to take it off to give me what I want.

Katrina gave Ferris a lascivious smile as she slinked toward him. "And what about what *I* want?"

"We'll get there," Ferris said with a wink. "But to start with, I think I need some payment for the good work I've done here."

Every now and then, I almost, just about, a tiny little bit, don't hate this guy…then he goes and behaves like this again.

They started off with what Ferris wanted, and then worked their way across each other's bodies for several minutes, and then Ferris pulled away and pushed himself across the room.

"Sorry, gotta use the san."

Katrina sighed, and winked at him. "Hurry."

Ferris had closed the door, and she was wondering if he'd know how to use a zero-*g* toilet when a message came in from Juasa over the maintenance-subsystem, and the tap into the comm array.

Her mental tone seemed scared, and her words were rushed. <*Katrina, if you can hear me, we have a—*>

The message cut off, and Katrina tried to reach out to Juasa.

There was no response; not directly, and not through their back channels.

<*Troy, I've lost contact with Juasa.*>

<*And I've just lost contact with the ship as a whole,*> Troy replied. <*Their network is still up, but it's refusing connections. Going to see if I can breach their security through your backdoor.*>

<*OK, I think it's time I took care of Ferris.*>

Troy made a gagging sound. <*Good, because with the way he treats you, even I want to kick his ass.*>

<*And they say chivalry is dead.*>

<*What's chivalry?*> Troy asked.

When Ferris exited the san, Katrina was waiting for him.

"Just can't keep away, is that it?" Ferris asked.

"Something like that," Katrina replied. She considered giving Ferris a speech about how he needed to treat women like equals and not leverage, but decided it wasn't worth it.

"Goodnight," was all she said before activating the nano she had inserted into his body on their first encounter.

Ferris's eyes widened, and he managed to utter 'whaa—' before he went limp.

Katrina guided Ferris's inert body into the stasis chamber across the corridor, and pushed him into one of the pods.

"Sorry, buddy, no stasis suit for you."

<*What's going on?*> Carl asked. <*I can't raise the* Havermere*, or anyone on it.*>

<*I got a cryptic message from Juasa,*> Katrina replied, trying to hide the worry from her mental voice. <*I think we were just double-crossed. I'm going to run an active scan on the* Havermere *and see if I can get any kind of read on things.*>

<*Shit! Are you serious? Is Ju OK?*> Carl asked frantically.

<I don't know if Ju is OK, I can't reach her at all. Any idea who might be behind…whatever is happening over there?>

Carl didn't even hesitate. *<My money is on Anna, shifty bitch. But this means that Mandy and Juasa are both stuck over there. How are we going to get them back?>*

<Carl,> Katrina said *<I'm going to need you to get this ship FTL capable in one hour.>*

<What?!>

<No a-grav, no dampeners, no shields. Focus only on FTL. One hour.>

<Katrina…we've never done it that fast. Like…not even close."

<You'll have to figure it out. I don't trust that we're dealing with just one enemy out there. If that was the case, Anna would have tried something sooner.>

<What do you mean?> Carl asked. *<Maybe she just wanted to find your ship first.>*

<Then she would have sent her people on the first shuttle over. She's buying time.> Carl didn't respond and Katrina pushed the point. *<Even if we're not sure, we have to assume she has help coming. And I need* ***you*** *to get us FTL capable.>*

<OK,> Carl said after a moment. *<I'll see what I can do.>*

<Carl!> Katrina said, her tone unforgiving. *<If we get captured, death may be something we crave before long. Don't 'see what you can do'. You do it. Whether we live or die is on your shoulders now.>*

<Fuck, Katrina, thanks. No pressure, right?>

Katrina didn't reply. Carl knew the stakes. Either he succeeded or he didn't. Either way, she needed more options.

<Troy,> Katrina asked as she reached the Flight Deck and settled into her seat. *<What are his chances of pulling it off?>*

<Toss up right now. If we were a ship from his time, sure, he could do it. But half the stuff he has needs custom adaptation to work with our power grid and network. I have the fab working overtime to get him what he needs, and the automatons too. Any time you can

add to the clock will be greatly appreciated. Oh, and try not to be such an ass—that's my job.>

Katrina blinked at the rebuke. <*You listening in on private conversations?*>

<*Right now, when our lives are on the line? Yes, I'm listening to everything.*>

Katrina bit back a response. Troy was right, he was almost always right. <*Sorry…just…I need to get Juasa safe.*>

<*I understand. I'm running the scan you were thinking about before you decided to chew Carl out. I still can't reach anyone aboard the* Havermere, *but there have been no signs of weapons fire or explosions, from what I can see.*>

<*What about the back door into their AI that I made?*> Katrina asked.

<*I'm working on it. They've shut down their beacon, and their comm array is offline, too. Trying to ping their sensors to see if I can create an overflow and get some sort of access. It's a long shot, though.*>

Katrina considered her options. If accessing the *Havermere*'s systems remotely was out of the question, she may have to go in and do things the hard way.

"Can you activate our stealth systems?" she asked aloud.

<*Not right now. I have the system that powers the rad benders offline—part of the power grid alterations we need to do.*>

Katrina sighed. "Stealth's probably not a good idea anyway, 'til we're under thrust. I don't really want to try our weapons against theirs, either. From what I understand, their grav shields can just bend our lasers away."

<*Two of our beams are x-ray; those may get through,*> Troy suggested.

"They have at least sixty beams on that ship. I don't think we'd make a dent with those two before they took ours out," Katrina replied.

<*Can't fight, can't run—yet. What are you thinking?*>

"Is the armor rack still powered up?"

<*Yes, it has its own backups in case of ship-wide failures.*>

"Good. I'm going to get armored up and go EVA across to the *Havermere*."

<*Katrina, you've lost your mind. Why are you taking this risk?*>

"Troy…We went on this crazy adventure to find a place where we belonged. To find someone special. Well…I have found someone."

<*We're trying to find the* Intrepid, *to find Tanis!*> Troy exclaimed. <*You're putting all that at risk.*>

"We might never find them," Katrina said softly. "You probably know the odds far better than I. But Juasa means something to me, and I can't just leave her behind."

Troy didn't respond as she pushed herself out of her seat and down the ladder shaft toward deck seven and the armory. As she approached the rack, he finally replied.

<*You're right. The odds aren't good. What do you need from me?*>

"Your support…and watch over Carl and the gang. This is going to get dicey."

CAPTAIN ANNA

STELLAR DATE: 11.17.8511 (Adjusted Gregorian)
LOCATION: KSS *Havermere*
REGION: Scattered Disk, Bollam's World System (58 Eridani)

"Sam," Anna said as she settled into the command chair on the *Havermere*'s bridge. "Any change on the *Voyager*?"

<*No,*> Sam replied over the bridge's network, the disdain in his voice palpable. <*They are trying to communicate with us, though. Should I reply, your majesty?*>

<*You'll want to curb that attitude, Sam,*> Anna said privately. <*Hemry added some interesting functions when he shackled you. Care to find out what it's like to have some of your memories erased?*>

<*You're a fucking bitch, Anna. This isn't going to work. KiStar, hell, the entire Space Force is going to come for you.*>

<*You're not thinking big picture, Sam,*> Anna said, letting a wry smirk grace her lips. <*I have no intention of staying in Bollam's. They can froth all they want, I'll be halfway across the Orion Arm, living like a queen.*>

"I have a ship on scan," Hemry said from one of the bridge consoles. "Profile looks like the *Verisimilitude*."

"About time," Anna said as she brought up the scan data on the bridge's main holodisplay. "Yeah, if that's not the *Verisimilitude,* I don't know what it would be. Buggers are an hour late, too. We could have this show on the road by now."

"Do you think that Verisa will surrender the *Voyager*?" Hemry asked, looking up and meeting Anna's eyes.

"What choice does she have? We outgun her, and she has no FTL. She can't run, she can't hide."

Hemry's expression grew clouded. "So long as she doesn't have any tech we don't know about."

Anna snorted. "If she did have an ace up her sleeve, don't you think she'd have played it by now?"

Hemry didn't reply and returned his gaze to the console before him, his expression showing more than a little uncertainty.

<*The* Verisimilitude *is hailing us,*> Sam said tonelessly. <*Should I put our new, dark overlords on?*>

"Yes, Sam. Now shut up."

The bridge's holodisplay changed from the view of the *Verisimilitude*'s exterior to that of its bridge. Anna's breath caught. She had expected some senior captain of the Blackadder to be in command of the ship, but it was none other than Jace Kaidan himself.

"You must be Anna," Jace said through his thick, red beard. "And I assume this ship off your port side is what you claim to be a Streamer vessel?"

Anna swallowed and nodded. "It is, Chieftain Kaidan. We've already pulled eight stasis pods from it; all of which we have confirmed to be the genuine article."

Jace arced an eyebrow. "Have you now? Stasis pods…just eight?"

Anna shook her head. "There were another half dozen or so in their hold, but there are probably more—being a Streamer ship."

"How certain are you of that? It looks like a Jasepsce model, perhaps an Imperial. Older, but still serviceable."

"Even if it is, the pods are still an incredible find," Anna said, wondering why Jace didn't seem impressed. Maybe he was just playing her to see what else she was holding back.

"True, true," Jace nodded. "Send the pods you have over here, and we'll inspect them."

"I'll send over one," Anna said. "Once you agree to a price, and the funds transfer, you'll get the rest."

Jace's dark eyes grew darker, but after a moment's consideration he nodded. "Very well. But send over the woman—the one you mentioned in your message that has leverage over the Streamer captain."

"Chieftain—" Anna began, but Jace cut her off.

"I am leaving you with the majority of the spoils, and taking you at your word that there is further bounty to be had. Send the woman. That is not negotiable."

Anna knew better than to argue the point. "Very well."

*****

Katrina kept her focus on the *Havermere* as she drifted through the black between the two ships.

Untethered EVA had been her least favorite part of her training in her youth, and she had managed to go her entire life never having to do it for real.

Until now.

She was still seven hundred meters from the *Havermere,* and thus far appeared to be undetected.

<*Any changes?*> she sent back to the *Voyager* on a tight-beam.

<*Yeah,*> Troy replied. <*That backup you figured they had? It's on its way.*>

<*Times like this, I really hate being right.*>

<*Me too,*> Troy said. <*If you try and be wrong real hard, do you think they might disappear?*>

Katrina ignored his comment. <*What kind of ship is it?*>

<*Its engine and powerplant mass are disproportionately large. I don't see much cargo capacity.*>

<*Bollam's military?*> Katrina asked.

<*I doubt it. Would they send just one ship?*>

Katrina resisted the urge to give her head a rueful shake—she didn't want to mess up her trajectory. <*No, if they even suspected we're a Streamer ship, they'd send the cavalry.*>

<*Oh, and their ETA is twenty minutes,*> Troy supplied.

<*Well, at least I'll be aboard the* Havermere *by then. If things get hot, you jump to the rendezvous. I can take control of the* Havermere *and meet you there.*>

Troy gave a snort. <*You've always had a high opinion of yourself.*>

Katrina chuckled. <*It's deserved.*>

<*You stay safe, Katrina. I promised Laura I'd look after you.*>

<*I made the same promise about you,*> Katrina replied.

They didn't speak further, and Katrina killed the connection to avoid detection. Five minutes later, she was nearly at the *Havermere*; she held off firing her retro-jets until the last minute, only managing to slow to one meter per second before hitting the hull with a loud clang.

Stars, I hope no one was around to hear that, Katrina thought as she activated her maglock boots and slowly walked across the ship to an auxiliary hatch.

The hatch would be sealed against any external access, but Juasa had disabled the locks yesterday. Hopefully no one had run any maintenance checks and spotted the change. If so, this would be one short rescue.

Katrina flipped open the manual keypad beside the hatch, and punched in the code Juasa had given her.

To her great relief, the access light turned green, and the hatch rotated ninety degrees and swung open. Katrina gauged the room in the small airlock to be just barely big enough for her powered armor, and carefully pulled herself in.

Moment of truth, she thought, and keyed in the command to cycle the airlock.

Air rushed into the enclosed space and, a minute later, the interior hatch on the airlock opened. Katrina crawled out into a—thankfully—empty maintenance tunnel.

Katrina swept the dark, narrow tunnel with her armor's sensors and confirmed that she was alone. Then she turned and quickly sealed the airlock before moving down the maintenance tunnel to the ship's bow.

* * * * *

Anna swept into the forward bay, the gleam of her silver skinsheath reflecting off the deck as she strode toward the shuttle.

It was still guarded by Kelly and Tali, as the unconscious form of Juasa was nearby.

She hoped the two women wouldn't question her change of clothing. With luck, they'd just assume that she didn't want to meet with the Chieftain of the Blackadder while in her tacky white KiStar uniform.

Which was actually the truth.

Anna considered that when this job was done, she could help herself to Verisa's wardrobe. The woman may have been a lying Streamer, hoarding all her tech, but she had a great sense of style.

"Get her in the shuttle," Anna ordered the two women as she approached.

"Who?" Kelly asked. "Juasa?"

Anna shook her head. "Yeah, shit-for-brains, Juasa. I'm taking her over to the *Verisimilitude*."

"What about the pods?" Tali asked, her brow lowering. "Should we unload them?"

Anna shook her head. "No, I'm taking them over, too."

"What? All of them?" Kelly asked.

"Yeah, all of them. That's Jace Kaidan over there on that ship. He wants all the pods, he gets all the pods. Don't worry, we'll get our cut."

Tali's eyes widened at the mention of Jace's name, but Kelly folded her arms and widened her stance.

"Blackadder are pirates. You take Ju and the pods, you take all our leverage with them."

"Oh, fuck it, I don't have time for this," Anna swore as she reached behind her back for the pistol tucked into her belt. She whipped it out, and fired three shots at Kelly, then pivoted to put two into Tali.

The weapon's report echoed through the bay, and a worker on the far side cried out in alarm. Anna fired a few shots in his direction, not bothering to see if she hit the man before reaching down and grabbing Juasa by the hair.

"Time to finally earn your keep, you stupid bitch." Anna muttered as she dragged Juasa onto the shuttle, and dropped her onto the deck. She considered securing the unconscious woman, but decided not to bother as she sat down at the small craft's controls.

<Everything OK down there?> Hemry asked from the bridge.

Anna ignored him as she fired up the shuttle's grav drive and lifted it off the docking cradle. Hemry pinged her again, insisting she give him an update.

She chuckled as she disconnected from the shipnet.

Suckers.

* * * * *

Katrina peered around a corner, checking that the coast was clear before moving into a corridor that would lead her to the main passageway between the forward and rear bays.

She decided to take the risk, and made a wireless connection to the shipnet; then she tapped into the maintenance subsystem. From there, she attempted to reach Juasa once more.

<*Juasa!*> Katrina called out, still getting no response. She searched, unable to find her on the shipnet at all. It wasn't as though she was sleeping, or unconscious—she just wasn't there.

Dammit! Katrina swore in her mind, feeling a frantic sense of urgency fill her as she moved as quietly as possible through the corridor. She should have worked out a way to bring Juasa on the first trip to the *Voyager.* Then they could have just boosted away, and activated the stealth systems.

That would have been a far better plan…

<*What is this?*> a voice asked, querying the tap she had placed in the subsystem.

Katrina realized that she had become sloppy, remaining connected to the subsystem after sending out her broadcasts. Before she could disconnect, the voice said, <*Please, I need your help. It's me, Sam.*>

Katrina wondered why Sam was reaching out to her like this. *Is this a ploy? To what end? The tap doesn't give away my physical location; not this quickly, at least.* She decided to chance a response.

<*What do you want, Sam?*>

<*Verisa! What are you doing here? They're after you, you know.*>

<*Who is?*> Katrina asked. <*Other than everyone.*>

<*Uh…well, yeah. Everyone. But specifically the Blackadder.*>

Katrina didn't need to guess who that was. <*The pirate ship out there. Anna sold me out to them, I assume?*>

<*Not just you. She sold* ***everyone*** *out. She's going to take Juasa and the pods over there and leave the* Havermere *high and dry.*>

Katrina had to give Anna credit. She wasn't taking half measures.

<*How come you're helping me?*> Katrina asked as she checked the cross corridors at an intersection before proceeding.

<Fuckers shackled me like I'm a damn non-sentient.>

<Now you know how half the people on this ship feel. How come you're able to talk to me like this, if you're shackled?>

Sam snorted. *<I didn't say they did a great job at it. Besides, your little hack here is ingenious. If anyone is monitoring me, it just looks like I'm reviewing maintenance systems.>*

<Thanks, I think.>

<Why are you still moving so slow?> Sam asked after a moment.

<Because I don't want to be seen.>

<Katrina, you misunderstand me. Anna is in the bay ***right now****. If you don't get there fast, she's going to leave with Juasa!>*

<Dammit, Sam!>

Katrina took off at a full run, banking around a corner and into the main passageway between the aft and forward docking bays. She careened off the wall, pushed an automated hauler aside, and burst past a group of crewmembers.

It was only four hundred meters to the forward bay, and she covered the distance in less than fifteen seconds. Bursting into the bay, she nearly collided with a fleeing man with blood running down his arm.

Her eyes landed on the empty cradles, and then caught sight of the shuttle passing through the grav shield and into space.

"No!" Katrina cried out, the armor triggering her external speakers and blasting the cry of anguish into the bay. Rage coursed through Katrina's body, and she looked for someone to take it out on. All she found were the bodies of two dead members of the crew.

<Sam! Was she on that shuttle?> Katrina demanded.

<She was; if you'd only started running when I told you—>

<You say one more stars-damned word, and I'll find your core, rip it out, and crush it under my boot. Do you hear me?>

Sam wisely did not respond as Katrina considered her options.

None came to mind.

An assault on the pirate ship would be suicide; it would be fully crewed with killers. Her only option was negotiation. She needed to get a message to Troy, and advise him of what she was planning.

<*Sam, turn on the* Havermere*'s comm array. I need to send a message.*>

<*I can't, that's a system I'm locked out of.*>

Katrina shook her head and made a connection to the hack that her nano had performed. It would take a minute to initialize, but what choice did she have?

The nano responded, and began to put into effect the bridge that would allow her to use the comm array without detection.

<*What are you—wow! You have really advanced nanotech,*> Sam commented as the bridge completed.

<*Yes, I know,*> Katrina snapped, unable to manage her temper. She activated the array, and was in the process of establishing a tight-beam to the *Voyager* when the deck beneath her feet shuddered, and the bay's lights went out.

<*We've been hit!*> Sam exclaimed.

Katrina didn't reply to him, and instead messaged Troy.

<*Anna took her, she's on a shuttle. What's going on out there?*>

<*That new ship—the* Verisimilitude*—just fired on the* Havermere.> Troy reported.

<*Just out of the blue?*> Katrina asked.

<*No, the* Havermere *fired on the shuttle—I guess the one with Juasa and Anna on board. The* Verisimilitude *returned fire. That ship has some high-powered weapons. It punched right through the* Havermere*'s shields and into the hull. Based on what's venting into space, I think that they hit the ship's power—*>

<*Troy, stop! The* ***shuttle****, is it OK?*>

<I think so. It took a glancing blow and vented atmosphere for a moment. Then suddenly it stopped. I think the pirate ship was able to extend its shield to encompass the shuttle.>

Katrina let out a long breath. There was still room for hope.

"You! Freeze!" a voice called out from the entrance to the bay. Katrina turned to see seven of the *Havermere*'s crew in the entrance. Six held pulse rifles, and the seventh hefted a railgun.

"Take it easy with the rail," Katrina said. "We could lose forward shields with another hit like we just took. You want to hole the hull and suck vacuum?"

"You come nice and slow, and we won't have to worry about that," the man with the railgun said.

Katrina surveyed her surroundings, and saw a stack of crates that contained hull plates. *Those should slow down whatever the rail fires—provided the label is correct and they haven't been repurposed.*

"Fat chance," Katrina retorted. She unslung her projectile rifle, sprayed rounds at the *Havermere*'s crew as she ran toward the stack, and then dove behind it.

Something pinged off her armor as she leapt. She landed on her side and flipped over, worried about what she would find. There was only a large dent in her thigh plate; the railgun must fire at a lower velocity than she'd feared—or they had dialed it back, also worried about holing the hull.

Still—that's gonna ache in the morning, she thought.

<Nice shooting! You got two of them,> Sam said.

The crates shook as high-powered rounds hit them, and Katrina shook her head. *<But not the guy with the rail, it seems.>*

<Oh, you took him out; one of his friends picked up the weapon.>

Katrina sent out a set of probes and saw that the enemy was only firing at the sides of the stack, hoping to catch her as she peered around while they slowly approached to flank her.

Such two-dimensional thinking.

She leapt onto the top of the crates and fired another salvo, taking out three more of the shooters before dropping back behind her cover.

When she hit the deck, it lurched, and for a moment, Katrina thought that she'd bent the plate with her powered armor. Then the floor beneath her shifted again, and she realized that the ship was moving.

<*Took another hit—inertial dampeners are offline,*> Sam advised.

<*Noted.*>

A moment later, the artificial gravity died, and the ship shifted again. Her armor's maglock boots held onto the deck, but the crates weren't strapped down and they slid toward her.

Katrina tried to get out of the way, but she wasn't fast enough and one of the crates slammed into her. Her maglock boots let go, and she flew into the bulkhead—the crate of hull plating following close behind. Katrina fired her armor's jets, getting clear an instant before the crate slammed into the place where her head had been.

The hull dented and Katrina could hear a slow hiss. It seemed the shields were now down entirely. Vacuum waited on the other side of that alloy.

On the far side of the bay, the *Havermere*'s crew weren't faring much better with the shifting cargo and flying tools—a situation made even more dangerous by their lack of armor.

The bay's a-grav systems wavered, creating a rollercoaster feeling in Katrina's stomach, and then failed altogether.

<*You need to get out of there,*> Sam said with only moderate urgency in his tone.

<*You're telling me,*> Katrina said as she fired her armor's jets to stabilize herself, and took aim at the enemy at the bay's entrance.

<The power's failing; the bay entrance's grav shield is about to shut down.>

Katrina took another shot at the man holding the railgun, and hit him in the right arm. The weapon fell to the deck, and she fired her jets at full power, streaking across the bay.

Behind her, the exterior door's grav shield began to weaken, and air began to seep through, creating an eerie whistling sound.

The three remaining members of the *Havermere*'s crew fired on Katrina as she approached, but the kick from their weapons made aiming impossible without gravity.

She barreled into one, and pushed another back, her maglock boots activating the moment her feet met the deck.

A second later, the exterior bay door's grav shield failed entirely, and a deafening *FOOM* thundered through the air. One of the men clamped his hands over his head, crying out in pain.

A torrent of air blew around her as the bay decompressed, and Katrina grabbed two of the men who had been firing at her a moment ago, and hauled them into the passageway, reaching its relative safety a second before the emergency pressure door slammed shut.

Katrina surveyed the corridor and saw two more of the *Havermere*'s crew: a man and a woman. Both had their hands clamped over their ears, as well. Their moans and mewling sounds filled the thin air.

They were no longer threats, and Katrina ignored them. She turned down the passageway and ran toward the lift.

<You still out there, Troy?> she asked.

<Yeah, but the Havermere *is listing. One of the bays blew out, and the ship is starting to spin.>*

<I know, I was in that bay.>

<You OK?> Troy asked.

Katrina had no idea how to answer that question, so she ignored it. <*Did the shuttle make it over safe?*> she asked instead.

<*'Safe' is a relative term, but yes; I believe the inhabitants were unharmed.*>

Small miracles, Katrina thought privately.

<*What's your plan?*> Troy asked.

<*I have no idea,*> Katrina replied. <*I thought maybe I'd try bluster. How's Carl and crew doing?*>

<*When the* Verisimilitude *arrived, they sure picked up the pace,*> Troy said. <*But I estimate they're still thirty minutes from us making a successful transition.*>

<*That's a lot of time to buy,*> Katrina replied.

<*Do what you can, but be careful—as much as you can.*>

Katrina was glad that Troy didn't try to convince her to come back—though she half-wished he would. She didn't see any way that this would end well.

*****

Consciousness slowly returned to Juasa, though she almost wished it hadn't. Everything hurt—a lot.

Her mouth throbbed with searing pain, and she tentatively felt her teeth. Two were loose, one was missing, and another was cracked. It felt like her jaw might be dislocated as well.

Scared to open her eyes, Juasa shifted and gasped in pain as something moved in her chest. She'd fractured ribs before, but this felt worse—they must be broken.

"Oh, you're awake?" a nearby voice asked.

Juasa knew it, but it took a moment for her to place it properly. "Anna," she whispered, careful not to move her jaw.

"Yup, that's me. Hold tight back there; you look like you're in pretty rough shape, if I have to shoot you, you may not survive."

"You bitch." Juasa packed all the venom she could into those two, soft words.

"That's me, the richest bitch you've ever seen," Anna laughed.

Juasa finally mustered up the courage to open her eyes. She was in the shuttle, on the floor at the entrance to the cockpit. Outside the glass was a starscape…and the growing shape of the *Verisimilitude.*

"What are you doing?" Juasa asked.

"'To the victor go the spoils', right?" Anna replied. "Well, I have all the spoils, so…."

Juasa didn't have the strength to reply, and closed her eyes again, trying to fight back tears. There was no way Katrina could help her now.

Unless…

I'm just a bargaining chip. They want Katrina.

"*Verisimilitude,*" she heard Anna say. "Come in. There's been a change of plans."

"You better not think you can double-cross me," a deep male voice replied.

"Jace, I'm more than just a pretty face. That's the last thing on my mind," Anna replied. "I don't have any intentions of sharing with the rest of the morons on that KiStar piece of junk. I'm bringing you *all* the pods, and I have the Streamer woman's girlfriend."

A short laugh came over the comm system. "You really sound like my kind of girl, Anna. Good work. Bay's open; bring 'em in."

"Be there in a minute," Anna replied.

A second later, a warning alarm sounded and the shuttle shuddered and slewed to the side.

"Fuck!" Anna yelled.

Juasa heard a whistling, and then a *foosh* as the cabin rapidly depressurized. Closing her eyes against the pain, she forced her jaw wide to open the canals to her ears, and then forced all the air out of her lungs.

A moment later, the torrent of air stopped; Juasa, her eyes still closed, wondered why the vacuum of space felt so…normal.

"Shit," she heard Anna swear faintly.

It's sealed? We still have air? Juasa wondered, and opened her eyes. No, she could see space through a rent in the hull. They must be inside the *Verisimilitude*'s shields; the pirates must have wrapped the shuttle in a bubble that would contain its atmosphere.

If not for the fact that the people who had just saved her were probably going to torture her, Juasa would be impressed. But as consciousness slowly drifted out of reach, she wished that space's cold vacuum had taken her life.

That would be far better than what was to come.

*****

Katrina reached the lift to the Command Deck, and gave it a moment's thought before turning to the ladder shaft that ran next to it. It didn't offer much cover, but it was better than stepping out of the lift into a barrage of weapons fire.

She climbed the ladder as quickly and quietly as she could, while around her, the ship groaned as it spun in space. She wondered how much damage it had taken from the pirate ship; was it in danger of breaking up?

Katrina slowed as she reached the command deck, and sent a probe ahead to confirm that the coast was clear.

It was not. As she'd feared, four enemy troops crouched behind makeshift cover with their railguns aimed at the lift doors. However, the command deck still had artificial gravity. That would be helpful.

She reached down to her waist, detached a flashbang grenade, and got ready to throw it. Just before she let it fly, the lift doors opened, and the four men and women let out bloodthirsty screams as they opened fire into the car.

<*You're welcome,*> Sam said as the grenade flew into the enemy's midst.

<*Thanks,*> Katrina said as she opened fire with her pulse rifle, dropping all four of the *Havermere*'s crew in moments.

Katrina stomped on their railguns as she passed by, destroying each of the weapons on her way to the bridge.

When she reached the sliding doors, Katrina reared back and kicked hard.

Once. Twice. On the third strike, the steel buckled. She grasped one of the doors and pulled with all her armor's might.

The door screeched in protest, and then broke free, flying down the corridor behind her. She leveled both her rifles and strode onto the bridge to find only Hemry, standing in front of the command chair with his arms raised in surrender.

"I didn't know!" he pleaded. "She fooled us all."

Katrina fired a round from her pulse rifle. The blast hit Hemry center mass and threw him across the bridge.

<*Sam?*> Troy asked as Katrina spun around, ensuring no other crew were hiding behind consoles.

<*Whoa, Who are you?*> Sam responded.

<*I'm Troy, the AI over on the* Voyager. *I've managed to get into the* Havermere's *systems via Katrina's comm hack.*>

<*Who's Katrina?*> Sam asked.

<*I am,*> Katrina replied as she sat in the command chair and brought up the comm logs.

<*Ohhhhhhh,*> Sam said. <*Subterfuge, I get it.*>

<*Great. Glad that you approve,*> Troy replied. <*I can remove the shackles they put on your core. Can I be assured of your cooperation?*>

Sam didn't respond for a moment. <*If I don't give it, will you put them back on?*>

<*No,*> Troy replied. <*I might kill you if you harm Katrina, but I won't shackle you.*>

Sam chuckled. <*Sounds fair. I give you my word.*>

"Hemry and some guy named Jace Kaidan sure had a fun chat," Katrina said as she reviewed the comm logs.

<*He's the leader of the Blackadder,*> Sam said before suddenly crowing in delight. <*Oh, stars…What did you do?*>

<*I unshackled you,*> Troy replied equitably.

<*No…this is different. Things have never been like this before,*> Sam replied.

<*Of course not. From my cursory examination, you've always been shackled.*>

<*No, I wa—Oooooo…. Those fuckers!*>

"Now's not the time," Katrina said. "We need a plan."

<*Incoming transmission,*> Sam said. <*It's Jace.*>

Katrina reached up, unsealed her helmet, and pulled it off. "Put him on."

The holodisplay on the bridge flickered for a moment, and then the figure of a broad-shouldered man with long red hair and a thick beard appeared.

"Well!" he said with a snort. "Either you're the woman I've been dying to meet, or Hemry has made a few well needed improvements to his looks."

Katrina narrowed her eyes and stood from the command chair. "My name is Katrina, and I demand that you turn Juasa over to me."

Jace chortled and waved his hand to the side. The view of the *Verisimilitude*'s bridge widened to show Juasa standing nearby—with Anna's arm wrapped tightly around her throat.

"Hi, Verisa…or I guess it's really Katrina? Juasa would say hi, but she's too focused on breathing right now."

Katrina's breath caught as she saw the look of fear in Juasa's eyes. Her face was bruised and smeared with blood and tears. A chunk of her dark hair was missing, and her once-pristine, white uniform was smeared with dirt and grime.

"As you can see, Katrina," Jace said, a toothy smile peeking out from behind his large beard. "I hold all the cards—many of which, Anna here was so kind as to bring with her."

"No problem," Anna said with a sweet smile. "I deliver."

Jace snorted a laugh as he glanced back at Anna. "You're a fun one, Anna. I can certainly see a place for you in my organization." He turned to face forward again. "You too, Katrina. Things got off to a bit of a rough start, but I can see that you're a resourceful woman. I respect that. I have use for resourceful people. I can protect you, too. A lot of places are like Bollam's World—all too eager to kill you and steal your tech."

"How's that different from you?" Katrina asked.

"Me?" Jace asked. "Well, I'll give you a job, a ship even—maybe even *your* ship over there, if we work things out right. That's a lot more than you would have received in this system."

<He's not wrong about that,> Sam commented privately. *<Well…provided he's not lying.>*

<Of course he's lying,> Troy replied.

Juasa let out a wavering gasp as Anna shifted, tightening her grip.

"Stop!" Katrina ordered. "You haven't seen what the *Voyager* can do. Let go of her, or I'll hole your ship through and through."

"Be my guest," Jace said with a magnanimous smile. "Take out the ship that your dear sweet lover is on. Sounds like a great plan. What other wonderful bits of bluster do you have stored up?"

<If you can get to a hatch on the port side of the Havermere, *I can pick you up,>* Troy said privately to Katrina. *<I think we can weather their beams long enough for you to get aboard. I can boost out on the AP drive, and then we can stealth. They'll never find us.>*

<I can't, Troy. I can't leave Juasa,> Katrina replied.

<Katrina, this was just a stop along the way; we still have a mission. We have to find the Intrepid. *I thought that was the thing you wanted most?>*

Katrina took a deep breath. So had she. *<I wanted to find friends. But here I've found love. Something that I thought I'd never have again. How could I abandon Juasa and live with myself? Everything would be hollow.>*

<You organics,> Troy said. *<Always thinking with your glands. What are you going to do?>*

<Buy more time…for you,> Katrina said.

Troy didn't respond.

"I don't have anything," Katrina replied to Jace, her voice sounding as dejected as she felt. "You win. What do you want?"

"For starters, I want you over here on the *Verisimilitude*. Then we'll talk about your ship, and how you're going to give me full control of it."

Katrina nodded slowly. "Will you let the *Havermere* be, if I do? They're fools, but they can do you no harm now."

Anna snorted. "You got that right. Pack of fools."

Jace shot a cold look back at Anna. "Shut up; the adults are talking." Anna's face reddened—a look that did not go well with her silver skinsheath.

<He'll kill you once he gets your ship,> Sam said. *<He'll kill Juasa, too.>*

<No. No he won't. He'll need us both.>

"Fine," Jace said after a moment. "I'll leave the *Havermere* alone. It'll amuse me to watch the feeds coming out of

Bollam's World. I'm sure that KiStar will have some very harsh things to say to its employees."

Katrina had no doubt about that. Still, it was the best they could hope for at present. She had no idea how much of the crew had participated in the mutiny, but hopefully some of them would get more justice from KiStar than they would from these pirates—that is, if Jace could be trusted. Which was hoping for a lot.

"Are you going to send a shuttle for me?" Katrina asked.

Jace laughed. "Why don't you just fly over in your armor? I imagine that's how you got on the *Havermere*."

"Sure," Katrina replied. "I'm almost out of fuel—it'll be fun. We'll see if I make it first."

"There's an escape pod on the port side of the bridge," Anna offered. "It has flight controls; you can fly it over here."

Jace shot Anna another look. "Helpful, but I told you to be quiet."

Anna's face reddened even further, and it looked like she was grinding her teeth. Perhaps Jace wasn't as accommodating a host as Anna had hoped.

"OK, I'm coming over," Katrina said. She killed the connection and picked up her helmet from where she had set it on the command chair.

Across the bridge, Hemry slowly rose to his feet, groaning as he straightened.

"Katrina, then, is it?" he asked, as he approached on shaking legs.

"Yes," Katrina replied. "Sam, you're in charge now. Get this ship somewhere safe. Once I get over there, I'll convince them not to shoot at you...somehow."

<*Real encouraging,*> Sam replied.

"Best I have," Katrina said. "Where's the pod Anna was talking about?"

<*Here,*> Sam said, and a panel slid open on the far side of the bridge.

"Thanks," Katrina said as she put on her helmet and walked across the bridge.

"So you're just going to leave to chase after Ju?" Hemry asked, his tone accusatory.

Katrina spun and took two loping steps to cross the bridge and stand face to face with Hemry, barely containing the urge to tear him in half.

"I have pretty much zero patience right now," Katrina hissed, her tone pure acid. "If you all hadn't been such greedy, entitled little pieces of human garbage, this would have all gone a lot differently. If I were you, I'd keep your mouth shut, or someone might just tear it off the donkey's ass you call a head."

Katrina turned and strode back across the bridge where she slid into the escape pod, and Sam whispered on the audible systems, "burnnnnnnnn."

She let a smile touch her lips at the AI's audacity, and then checked the seal on her helmet before triggering the pod's door to close.

<*Good luck,*> Sam said. <*OK, three, two, launch!*>

The escape pod rocketed out of the *Havermere*, and Katrina brought up the simple control interface, and directed the craft toward the *Verisimilitude.*

<*Katrina. Please, return to the* Voyager*; this is insane,*> Troy said, his message coming in on a tight-beam.

<*Troy, please stop. I have to do this. I can't be me otherwise.*>

<*You can't beat them,*> Troy said. <*Not an entire ship. They'll be ready for you.*>

<*I know,*> Katrina replied.

<*Then what are you doing?*>

<*Troy,*> Katrina said, her mental tone wavering. <*Troy, I'm buying you time to get out of here. That's all I can do now. You*

know that. When the time comes, as soon as you're ready, you need to go to FTL. Get out of here. Find the Intrepid.>

<*Katrina, we didn't do all this so you could sacrifice yourself like you're in some tragic human play,*> Troy said, and Katrina was surprised to hear the pleading tone in his voice. <*I* ***need*** *you here.*>

<*Carl and his people are good,*> Katrina said. <*Help them and they'll help you. I bet they'd* ***love*** *to see the* Intrepid.>

Ahead, a bay door opened on the *Verisimilitude,* and Katrina steered the escape pod toward it, firing the retro-jets as she approached.

<*Please, Katrina,*> Troy pleaded. <*It's not too late.*>

<*It is, Troy,*> Katrina said. <*I screwed this all up, but you don't have to go down with me. I'll always think of you fondly. Even if you are the biggest non-organic asshole that ever was. You jump as soon as you can. As soon as you're ready, you go. That's an order.*>

<*Katrina, you don't ord—*>

Katrina cut the connection. She knew what Troy was going to say, and she needed to focus. She had to get her head in the game. Jace was going to be ruthless, and she still had to come up with some way to get Juasa free.

She took slow, steady breaths as she approached the *Verisimilitude,* and recited her mantra to herself.

I am Katrina. Daughter of the despot Yusuf, friend of the Noctus, liberator of the Hyperion, *wife of Markus, president of Victoria…*

She paused, considering what came next, and then added, *lover of Juasa, and still searcher in the dark,* before continuing.

I am all of those things; together, they are me. They form my foundation; they give me purpose. My memories are my strength, the proof of my convictions.

I am the soft reed that grows along the shore. One foot in the river, one on land. I bend in the wind, I weather the flood, I persist, I survive. I touch all these things, I live in their worlds, but they are not me, and I am not them. I am Katrina.

The pod passed into the ship, and a grav beam caught hold of it and lowered it to the deck. Katrina pulled up the external feeds and saw that a dozen armored figures were arrayed in a semicircle in front of the pod. There was no sign of Jace or Juasa.

She triggered the pod's hatch and carefully stepped out, keeping the bulk of the pod—which only came up to her shoulders—between her and the enemy.

"Drop your weapons," one of the armored figures, a man in the center, called out.

"No," Katrina replied. "I want to see Juasa!"

"She's right here," another voice said, and Katrina saw the armored pirates part to allow their leader through.

One of Jace's hands gripped Juasa by her hair, and the other held a pistol to her neck. Juasa was crying, but when her soft hazel eyes met Katrina's, she drew a deep breath and straightened, nodding slightly.

"Oh, how sweet," Jace said with a coarse laugh. "She's all happy to see her mistress…or bitch? No. Mistress. Katrina is definitely the one on top in your pairing."

"Let her go, Jace," Katrina said. "Let her get in the pod; she can return to the *Havermere.* You have me."

"Almost," Jace nodded. "But you're a bit too well armed for my liking. Drop the weapons."

"Like I said." Katrina kept her tone as even as possible while looking into Juasa's fear-stricken eyes. "She goes first."

"And like *I* said," Jace said, punctuating each word with a pull on Juasa's hair, wrenching her head back and forth. "Take off your armor!"

As the bearded pirate screamed the last word, he lowered his pistol and fired a round into Juasa's side. The shot blew clear through, and blood poured out of the wound and down her dirty KiStar uniform.

Juasa screamed and held a hand to her side. Then Jace fired another round into her leg, and she collapsed, shrieking in pain as blood began to pool around her on the deck.

"I'm done playing games," Jace said in a soft voice. "I didn't mean to hit a vital in her gut, but I suspect I may have done just that. You cooperate, and we'll patch your lovergirl up. Fuck with me, and I'll still patch her up, just to shoot the shit out of her all over again. How's that sound? Or, you can drop your weapons…and take off your *fucking armor!"*

Katrina didn't hesitate this time. She tossed her two rifles aside, and then passed the command for her armor to unfold around her. Once all the sections had opened, she stepped out and glared at Jace.

"Now get her some help."

"I know a damn thermal-ballistic sub-layer when I see one," Jace said. "Take it off."

Katrina pulled the seal down on the sub-layer and stepped out of it. She was still wearing her black and red skinsheath, and Jace chortled at the sight of her.

"I should have known you'd dress like a Boller floozy."

"Help her," Katrina pleaded as the pool of blood slowly grew around Juasa.

Jace nodded at one of the soldiers, who stepped forward and sprayed a canister of biofoam into Juasa's wounds before picking her up and carrying her away.

"She'll be all right," Jace said with a grin. "If we have to, we can just put her in a stasis pod, too. Pop her out and let her die a bit more each time you act up. Those things are going to be so handy. I wonder what other lovely toys you have on your ship."

"You're a real fucker, you know that, Jace?" Katrina said through gritted teeth.

Jace laughed. "Yeah, I really am." He glanced at his soldiers. "Secure her."

Katrina readied herself as two of the soldiers approached, one on each side. When they were half a meter away, she leapt at the first one, depositing a dose of nano onto his armor, and then spun behind him, ready to do the same to the other.

The second soldier lunged for her, and Katrina grabbed his wrist, sending a passel into the joint. She was about to duck back behind the escape pod when a pulse blast hit her, sending Katrina flying across the deck.

She rolled to a stop and struggled to her feet, only to have another crushing shockwave slam into her body, and knock her down once more.

"Collar her," Jace called out, and Katrina heard the sound of boots hitting the deck growing louder as she pulled herself to her hands and knees.

Something cold touched the back of her neck, and then clasped around her throat. She reached a hand up to it, prepared to use a passel of nano to open the collar, when a punishing shock coursed through her body.

EM burst, she thought as a blinding headache overcame her.

"Do you like that?" Jace said as he approached. "I know that you Streamers—at least ones from far back enough to have stasis pods—are pretty tricked out. I had my squints make up this collar special for you. It'll fry your nano any time you try to use your tech—probably start to damage your nervous system after a while, too." Jace laughed, and she felt a boot press against her butt. "You'll probably want to behave."

Katrina couldn't form words. Everything hurt too much, and she fell to the deck, gasping for breath under the weight of Jace's boot on her.

She heard scuffling around her, and things went dark and then light again as consciousness came and went. She wasn't sure how long it lasted. It felt like hours, but it must have just been minutes.

Suddenly she was pulled to her feet, and an open palm slammed into her face, startling her awake. Her eyes snapped open, and she was staring into Jace's bearded face, only centimeters from her own.

"What did you do? Where did it go?" Jace screamed.

Katrina managed a slight smile.

Troy…you and Carl did it. Good job, guys. Go find Tanis….

"That ship doesn't have FTL! There's no way they could have upgraded it that fast!" Jace yelled.

"Apparently there is," Katrina whispered.

Jace turned to address someone next to him. "Has the team hit the *Havermere* yet?"

"Yes, Chieftain. They've just secured the bridge."

"At least there's that," Jace replied sourly. "Could be that they have other goodies from this bitch's ship. Space force is sending a scout ship to see what the ruckus is about out here, though. Tell them to jump it out to the rendezvous. At the very least, we'll have a new ship and some meat for the mill."

He turned back to Katrina, his eyes narrowing. "You and I are going to have a number of long chats about where your ship went, and about all the tech you have in that pretty little head of yours."

Katrina mustered up the courage to spit into Jace's face, and had the pleasure of watching the spittle run into his beard before he tossed her to the deck.

"Put her in one of her pods. There's no way she can cause any trouble in stasis."

Katrina struggled to rise, and took a swing at the first person that approached her; or at least she thought it was a person. She was seeing double of everything.

Someone laughed, and then another pulse blast hit her, slamming her back into the deck, and darkness returned.

ESCAPE

STELLAR DATE: 11.17.8511 (Adjusted Gregorian)
LOCATION: *Voyager*
REGION: Scattered Disk, Bollam's World System (58 Eridani)

Stupid human! Troy thought as Katrina severed the connection.

There was no logic in her actions. She couldn't save Juasa. Now that pirate would have both of them—and the *Voyager,* too, if they didn't get the graviton emitters working.

<*Carl, that's four-phase power, you have to convert it to three,*> he advised as he checked in on the engineer.

"Yeah, I know that, Troy!" Carl snapped. "I'm just getting everything situated. Kirb is picking up another converter from your fab shop. Once we get this one working, we should have enough to do the whole field.

Three emitters, when Carl's initial plan called for five.

From what Troy understood of the dark layer, it was a place of absolute nothing—except for dark matter, which you wanted to avoid colliding with at all costs. Staying in that nothing required creating a special gravitational field, mixed in with some rather intriguing forms of exotic energy.

If Troy didn't have the evidence of his own sensors witnessing so many ships appearing and disappearing, he would have dismissed the dark layer transition as utter nonsense.

She's been over there for too long already, Troy thought. *Soon he'll start torturing her for access to the* Voyager's *command systems…*

Unless we go.

He hated that Katrina had sacrificed herself. Hated it. For a woman she had just met, no less. Troy thought that *he* had meant something to Katrina. She had saved him from death on

Victoria's moon…he had stayed with her for decades, been her constant companion.

This was *their* quest, *their* mission.

And then she told him to carry on alone. Troy knew folly when he saw it, and what Katrina had just done was utter folly. Still, he would not abandon her. Once they had FTL, he would follow these pirates, and work up a strategy to take them down and free Katrina.

"OK," he heard Carl say. "Converter is in place. We have three-phase power.

<*About time,*> Troy replied.

"And just when I thought there couldn't be an AI grumpier than Sam," Kirb muttered.

<*Are we ready, then? To transition?*> Troy asked.

"Yeah," Carl replied. "But you understand about vector, right? You have to boost on the path I provided, or we'll drift into a field of dark matter."

<*I understand the concepts and dangers,*> Troy replied.

"Good," Carl said. "OK, I'm activating the field."

Troy fired the attitude jets, then fired a burst from the *Voyager*'s AP drive and signaled to Carl to perform the transition.

"Here goes nothing…" Carl said nervously.

Troy detected gravitons surrounding the ship, and a bubble of sorts snapped into place. Then the stars were gone.

"It worked," Carl cried with delight, and Troy watched him slap Kirb on the back. Rama and Camille were cheering from their stations at the other emitters, and Troy felt like cheering, too.

Except that it meant they were leaving Katrina behind.

He was about to congratulate Carl on a job well done, when a spike registered on the power grid. One of the power converters was drawing too much energy.

Carl saw it too. "Damn, gotta power it down, or we're gonna twist."

Troy had seen images of twisted ships, and had no desire to experience that. Before Carl could drop them out of the dark layer, Troy activated the stealth systems, praying that they would mask the ship the instant it returned to normal space-time.

When the stars snapped back into place, Troy performed some rapid triangulation, and was amazed to see that the ship had moved over a hundred thousand kilometers.

He directed passive scan toward the *Verisimilitude* and the *Havermere,* seeing that both ships were still present.

Then the *Havermere*'s engines flared, pushing the ship forward before it disappeared. Gone into the dark layer. A moment later, the *Verisimilitude*'s engines also came to life, and the ship accelerated on a course toward the *Voyager.*

Troy checked the stealth systems. They passed systems tests. There was no way that the *Verisimilitude* could see them. Yet the pirate vessel continued to approach, boosting as though it was trying to achieve ramming speed.

It closed within fifty thousand kilometers—then forty, thirty, twenty. As it was passing by the ten thousand kilometer mark, Carl burst into the cockpit.

"Do they see us? I thought you said this thing had some sort of stealth tech!"

<*They can't, and it does,*> Troy replied, his mental tone conveying far more conviction than he felt.

"Yeah, well it sure looks like it can—" Carl's words cut off in mid-sentence as the *Verisimilitude* disappeared. "Well, I'll be…they were getting more *v* before dumping to the DL…just happened to be on a vector right for us."

<*Unnerving, to say the least.*>

"So, what now?" Carl asked. "I know I just met you, but we're kinda stuck together for now."

<I just met you too, Carl,> Troy said dryly. *<But you seem like an honest and trustworthy man. Are you a trustworthy man?>*

"Uhhh…I like to think so," Carl replied. "What are you getting at?"

<How do you feel about a little rescue operation?>

Carl smiled. "I feel like you and I are on exactly the same page."

<I'm glad to hear it,> Troy replied. *<However, we'll still need FTL.>*

"Yeah," Carl nodded. "And now that we're not rushing around while shitting ourselves with fear, we'll get it right."

<Take your time, Carl. Well, not too much time.>

Carl shook his head. "Yeah, I know what you mean. We owe those girls a lot. Not gonna let them get…whatevered…"

<Agreed,> Troy said. *<No whatevering. Now let's get to work.>*

HOMEWORLD

STELLAR DATE: 12.25.8511 (Adjusted Gregorian)
LOCATION: UNKNOWN
REGION: UNKNOWN

"Katrina," a soft voice whispered.

Katrina heard the voice, heard the word, but it didn't register as anything she needed to concern herself with.

"Katrina," the voice whispered again, more urgently this time.

She turned over, tucking her head under her arm; whatever the voice wanted, it could wait. She was tired and she ached—ached *everywhere*. *Just a little more sleep*.

"Katrina, wake up, it's Juasa." A hand touched her shoulder, gently stroking her arm.

Suddenly, recognition surged through Katrina, and her eyes snapped open. She turned her head toward the sound of Juasa's voice. A smile spread across her dry lips, and she reached out a hand.

"Juasa…I had a terrible dream. You were shot."

Juasa gave a pained smile. "That was no dream, Kat. I was shot."

Katrina pulled herself up to a sitting position, only now realizing that she was on some sort of dirt—or maybe sand—floor.

Juasa was wearing a simple white shift, and Katrina reached out to touch her side. "Are you…OK?"

"Yes," Juasa said with a slow nod. "That was over a month ago. They patched me up, and I'm better now."

"A month," Katrina whispered, looking around at the small chamber they were in. The floor was stone, covered in dirt and sand. The walls were stone as well, and a steel door was set into one of them. "Where are we?"

Juasa sighed. "Hell."

Katrina looked down at herself to see that she too was wearing a simple white shift. "What do you mean?" she asked.

"This is Jace's castle," Juasa said after a moment.

"Castle?" Katrina asked, barely able to assign the utterance any credence. "We're in a castle?"

Juasa nodded. "I think so; we just got here yesterday. Took a while, too. I think we're on some planet…maybe thirty light years from Bollam's World. I'm guessing it's where he has his headquarters."

"In a castle."

"I don't know, Kat. Look around, it looks like a castle, right?"

Katrina took a deep breath, trying to get her bearings, when a loud clang sounded in the small room. Both women turned to watch the door open. A glowing, golden figure stepped into the cell, and Katrina shaded her eyes from the bright light. The intensity of the glow pouring off the person slowly diminished, until at last Katrina could make out Anna's grim smile.

Katrina groaned while Juasa rose, her hands clenched into fists. "Anna," she hissed. "I'm going to kill you for this."

"Really?" Anna asked, while putting her hands to her chest, an expression of mock fear on her face. "Be fun to watch you try. But for now, why don't you two come with these two large men? It's time to start your training."

Anna stepped out of the cell, and two men entered, one after the other. They were so large that Katrina wondered if they were human, or some sort of over-muscled automaton.

"C'mon," one said in a deep voice. "Time to earn your keep."

Juasa looked at Katrina, her eyes wide. "Kat, what are we going to do?"

"Don't worry," Katrina whispered as they walked out of the cell. "I'll figure something out."

THE END

*****

Katrina's story in the 86th century is just beginning, and she has a long road ahead before she finds the *Intrepid*.

A road that will require a fight for her freedom and her very survival at the hands of Jace Kaidan and the Blackadder.

Pre-order The Woman Who Seized an Empire on Amazon.

Learn more about the books of Aeon 14, and the ideal reading order, in the free Aeon 14 Reading Guide.

THANK YOU

If you've enjoyed reading *The Woman Without a World,* a review on Amazon.com and/or goodreads.com would be greatly appreciated.

To get the latest news and access to free novellas and short stories, sign up on the Aeon 14 mailing list: www.aeon14.com/signup.

M. D. Cooper

THE BOOKS OF AEON 14

The Intrepid Saga
- Book 1: Outsystem
- Book 2: A Path in the Darkness
- Book 3: Building Victoria

- The Intrepid Saga Omnibus – *Also contains Destiny Lost, book 1 of the Orion War series*

- Destiny Rising – *Special Author's Extended Edition comprised of both Outsystem and A Path in the Darkness with over 100 pages of new content.*

The Orion War
- Book 1: Destiny Lost
- Tales of the Orion War: Set the Galaxy on Fire
- Book 2: New Canaan
- Book 3: Orion Rising
- Tales of the Orion War: Ignite the Stars Within (Fall 2017)
- Tales of the Orion War: Burn the Galaxy to Ash (Winter 2018)
- Book 4: The Scipio Alliance (Nov 2017)
- Many more following

Perilous Alliance (Expanded Orion War - with Chris J. Pike)
- Book 1: Close Proximity
- Book 2: Strike Vector
- Book 3: Collision Course (October 2017)

Rika's Marauders (Age of the Orion War)
- Prequel: Rika Mechanized
- Book 1: Rika Outcast
- Book 2: Rika Redeemed (Nov 2017)
- Book 3: Rika Triumphant (2018)

Perseus Gate (Age of the Orion War)
- Episode 1: The Gate at the Grey Wolf Star
- Episode 2: The World at the Edge of Space
- Episode 3: The Dance on the Moons of Serenity
- Episode 4: The Last Bastion of Star City
- Episode 5: The Toll Road Between the Stars (Nov 2017)
- Episode 6: The Final Stroll on Perseus's Arm (Dec 2017)

The Warlord (Before the Age of the Orion War)
- Book 1: The Woman Without a Country
- Book 2: The Woman Who Seized an Empire (Dec 2017)
- Book 3: The Woman Who Lost Everything (2018)

The Sentience Wars: Origins (With James S. Aaron)
- Book 1: Lyssa's Dream
- Book 2: Lyssa's Run (Oct 2017)
- Book 3: Lyssa's Flame (Jan 2018)

Tanis Richards: Origins
- Prequel: Storming the Norse Wind (In At the Helm Volume 3)
- Book 1: Shore Leave (Fall 2017)

The Sol Dissolution
- The 242 - Venusian Uprising (In The Expanding Universe 2 anthology)
- The 242 - Assault on Tarja (In The Expanding Universe 3 anthology – coming Dec 2017)

The Delta Team Chronicles (Expanded Orion War)
- A "Simple" Kidnapping (Pew! Pew! Volume 1)
- The Disknee World (Pew! Pew! Volume 2)
- A Fool's Guide to Fangs and Food (Pew! Pew! Volume 3)

ABOUT THE AUTHOR

Michael Cooper likes to think of himself as a jack-of-all-trades (and hopes to become master of a few). When not writing, he can be found writing software, working in his shop at his latest carpentry project, or likely reading a book.

He shares his home with a precocious young girl, his wonderful wife (who also writes), two cats, a never-ending list of things he would like to build, and ideas…

Find out what's coming next at http://www.aeon14.com

CPSIA information can be obtained
at www.ICGtesting.com
Printed in the USA
BVOW03s1937211217
503400BV00001B/91/P